P9-CRK-328

A Jamaican Storyteller's Tale

Lorrimer A. Burford

LMH Publishing Limited

© 2005 Lorrimer Burford
First Edition
10 9 8 7 6 5 4 3 2 1

All rights reserved. No part of this book may be reproduced, stored in a retrieval system, or transmitted in any form or by any means, electronic, mechanical, photocopying, recording or otherwise, without the prior written permission of the publisher(s) or author(s).

If you have bought this book without a cover, you should be aware that it is "stolen" property. The publisher(s)/ author(s) have not received any payment for the "stripped" book, if it is printed without their authorization.

All LMH titles, imprints and distributed lines are available at special quantity discounts for bulk purchases for sales promotion, premiums, fund-raising, educational or institutional use.

Edited by *Charles Moore*
Cover Design by *Chris Loper for the Quantum Group*
Book Design & Layout by *Michelle Mitchell - Page Services*

Published by LMH Publishing Ltd.
Suite 10, 7 Norman Road
Kingston, C.S.O.
Jamaica, West Indies
Tel: 876-938-0005/0712
Fax: 876-759-8752
Email: lmhbookpublishing@cwjamaica.com
Website: www.lmhpublishingjamaica.com

Printed in the U.S.A.   ISBN 976-8184-84-1

Dedication

To my wife, Joyett, for your love and support.

Table of Contents

Chapter 1

I still remember that Friday in the summer of forty-five when my father marched through the door. Everyone, including my mother, realized something was different about him. He still wore the same old clothes and the silly grin peculiar to Lester Jenkins but this was definitely not the man who left home a few hours earlier. He held his head high in an engaging, 'I am the boss', manner we've never seen before.

"Sit down, Lester," my mother snapped, "no sense in you standing there like a stooge."

He sat down mockingly, exaggerating every movement to make sure my mother noticed. She watched him carefully, folding her arms under her bouncy breasts in the lethal female gesture he knew so well. Her face was wrinkled in a frown and her voice rushed. Watching her, he knew he was in for one of her usual tongue-lashings and the old fear briefly grappled at his chest. But yet, he sat still, waiting.

"You lazy devil you! Where have you been from morning? Coming in here like you're some big shot or other."

"Isabel…"

"Lester from morning you don't feed the pigs. Feed the pigs nuh man!"

Then, he stood up in a way he had never done before.

"Shut yuh mout' woman! All a yuh life yuh nuh give a man a chance fi seh what 'im have to seh."

"Lester," she squawked, rolling her eyes and stomping her oversized feet, "how much time I have to tell you, speak proper English in front of the children?" Then in a deprecating whisper, she said, "Damn negrish way of talking."

"To hell wid English," he shot back, pushing out his chest in exaggerated confidence, "Mi get chu!" Then he could hold the excitement no longer, jumping gleefully like a little boy who had just got his first real toy.

My father repeated over and over, "Mi get chu. Yes Isabel, mi get chu."

My mother stared at him quizzically for a moment as if unsure of what he was saying, fearing this was one of his jokes. "Dem accept yuh fi true Lester?"

"Yes Isabel, a Port Maria mi a come from. Di lady in a di Farm Work office say, a nex' week wi a leave fi Florida."

She held out her arms in jubilation and he went forward into her bosomy embrace. It was a comic sight, this diminutive five-foot-seven black man hugged firmly by his two hundred and ten pound gargantuan wife, his head partly hidden in her deep cleavage and encircled by her fleshy arms. It was also one of those rare occasions when my parents showed public affection, especially in front of my sister and me. We were momentarily stunned. Mother pushed him away from her, holding both his shoulders in a tight grip at arms length.

"You really, really get through?"

"Yes. Wi leavin' Monday week."

"Exactly where yuh going?"

"One a di worker dem tell mi seh is a place name Bellglade in a Florida. Dem call it di cane belt."

"Praise di Lord! God answer prayers fi true. You t'ink is now I been praying for you? Thank you again Jesus."

"Tell yuh di trut' Isabel, me nah look forward to go cut no cane. Me a go mek life fi you and di children dem. As soon as mi get di chance, mi a lef' di farm work and come fi unno."

"I hope is not duppy story on yuh mind Lester. You can't mek money a tell people duppy story."

"Mi know dat. We have fi fine somet'ing else fi do. Maybe start up a likkle shop or store an' mek some money. But mi have fi tell mi likkle story dem. A my legacy dat."

She moved closer and spoke forebodingly to him.

"Well Lester, just don't forget us. God will bless you. Yuh hear me husban'? May the good Lord keep and guide you."

Daddy left the following Monday and we never saw him again until three years later.

When I saw him, he looked older than his thirty-three years but he never looked better, neatly dressed, wearing black pants and a dark brown jacket even though the day was terribly hot. The sweat poured off his sun-drenched face, soaking his yellow and brown plaid shirt. Daddy hardly seemed to notice the heat as he hugged and kissed us all.

"Me glad fi see unno," he whispered with pleasure, "mi likkle girl, how yuh do? Son yuh seem fi grow so big in a di short space a time."

"Isabel mi sugar plum, come give mi a hug nuh? Me glad fi see yuh."

"Lester, stop it. You come back from foreign with your same old, dirty Jamaican patois? You can't do better man? Speak proper English in front of the children! How yuh expect them to learn if you don't train them yourself? Remember if you can't dance a yard you can't dance abroad."

Despite this tirade mother was delighted to see him. She just couldn't resist commanding him to speak proper English as a matter of habit. She hugged and kissed him in our presence for the first time, which embarrassed my sister and me very much, though we never showed it.

That Christmas of nineteen forty-seven was not about the presents he gave us, it was the reality that the entire family was going to America. In those days, it was unusual for more than two members of a family to leave at the same time for 'foreign'. But Daddy had saved enough money and, through a lawyer, secured visas and passage for my mother, my sister, and me. Only uncle Roger was left to take care of the house.

We arrived in the town of Belle Glade (at the time locals called it Hillsboro), one very cool January day nineteen hundred and forty eight. I still remember the short pants I wore with a thin brown belt tightened at its oversized waist, causing the pant's front to gather together like a skirt. My thin thighs and big knees jutted out from its enormous legs. At eight, I had grown to really hate short pants. My mother, on the other hand, said that I was a child and no 'pickney boy' would ever wear long pants in her house.

My chubby little five-year-old sister Pamela was thrilled by her brand new, bright yellow dress under which she wore the widest white crinoline I have ever seen. Had it not been for the ninety-two pounds on her four foot three body, she might have been mistaken for Cinderella. Of course, her feet were not as tiny or dainty as Cinderella's and the dress was far too yellow, but her pretty face could make her pass.

Mother must have been the proudest and happiest person in our group. I had never seen her show so much affection to father in her entire life. She was proud of the black and white broad brimmed hat with the white mesh my father had bought her. She wore it with the black stripe dress she stitched last summer. Everyone said the dress made her look slimmer, which delighted her, even though it hung from her round bottom like a sheet, threatening to sweep the very ground she walked on.

We settled in with the help of our neighbours, the Bensons. Mr. and Mrs. Benson were African Americans who had lived in Belle Glade all their lives. They were poor people who depended on cane season when Mr. Benson worked as a cane cutter to feed the family. I soon got to be good friends with their son, Joseph, who was my age. They had two other daughters Terry, seven, and Sheila who was sixteen. I remember now that it was Mrs. Benson who introduced my mother to Carmen Wright, a pretty American black lady who worked in a store downtown Belle Glade. She was very skinny and could pass for a white lady. On the other hand, everyone knew she was black because, although her mother was white, her father was a black man from a big city called New York. Miss Carmen and my mother became the best of friends and she was always at our house.

When we arrived in Belle Glade in nineteen forty-eight, the population of the area was about seven thousand permanent residents and growing rapidly. I wasn't used to seeing so many white people and knew nothing about segregation. Back home, as children, we used to quarrel amongst ourselves; the fair-skinned children cursed the dark-skinned ones, telling them they were 'black like tar'. The dark-skinned ones retaliated calling their antagonists 'mulattoes, red like puss'. This was the extent to the racial prejudice we experienced as children.

In Jamaica, especially in Highgate, we believed rich people lived separately from the poor people and behaved as if they were better but in Belle Glade, it was a world segregated across racial lines. Downtown Belle Glade was owned outright by whites as their businesses lined Main Street. Second Avenue was the mecca of black life, it was called black quarters and was where one would find all black enterprises.

Blacks also lived in residential areas separate from those of whites. The canal, which ran eastwards from Lake Okeechobee, separated the black territories from those of the whites. Coming from rural Jamaica, we were surprised to see that farms were owned by the whites, while blacks worked as laborers. This caused strained relationships between the groups. As a rule, black laborers thought they were being underpaid for their work in the fields and it was not unusual to see all the workers walking off the job in protest.

That was one of the reasons why daddy hated the cane fields and, that winter, he made up his mind never to cut cane again. By June, daddy opened a shop which sold sugar, bread, spices and other food products and swore never to cut cane again.

"Isabel," he said one day, "neva in me whole life me eva work so hard like when mi work inna di cane fiel'. Me nah do it again, but di pickney dem haffi go a school. Yuh will help mi in di shop, eh?"

"What's wrong with you Lester? Even here in America, where everyone speaks properly, you refuse to even try to talk good. You don't feel bad eh? Only you and the low class Jamaicans dem keep up this fool, fool patois, like unno still in Jamaica."

"Isabel, it nuh matta where mi live, a patois me ago talk all di time. But cho mi baby, nuh mind mi, jus' help mi run di likkle shop."

"How about Cecil, eh? Don't you see it affect him? All of the children in his school speak properly. You and your patois is holding him back."

"Di boy ago turn a great storytella like 'im faada and 'im granpappy. Yuh don't have fi worry 'bout 'im."

"Yuh mad Lesta? Yuh nuh have nuh ambition for yuh children? You ever earn a penny off storytelling in your whole life?"

"No, but wi never dead fi hungry and mi neva t'ief yet. Di boy wi' manage. Jus' watch."

"Lesta please," she pleaded, as she had done many times before, "give the boy a chance, mek wi help him through school."

"Mek me tell yuh somet'ing Isabel, me nuh stop 'im from go a school and me nuh want 'im fi come cut no cane, but a nuff good trade di bwoy can learn an' still tell 'im story."

Mama sighed in resignation and her large breasts heaved as she breathed heavily in disgust. She hissed her teeth long and hard, and then retreated. *Another time, she thought, I'll have to make the stubborn fool understand our son has to become a doctor, or a lawyer, or something we can be proud of, but definitely not a storyteller.* Mama helped him in the shop and she enjoyed it very much.

I really grew to like Belle Glade. Once my father decided to open his own business and move away from the black quarters of town, good things began to happen to us. Although we stayed on the black side of Belle Glade, we were able to live like we used to in Jamaica. Soon, Mama's friend, Carmen, bought a house close to us and other Jamaicans began building houses close by. In a short time, the area had a decent mix of Jamaicans, African Americans and other Caribbean folks living close together. A few Native Americans had been living there long before us and we got to be friendly with some of them especially the Kaneohes, a family of two boys, their mother and father.

It seemed like us Jamaicans carried our customs and lifestyle with us wherever we went. We planted little gardens with produce such as peas, tomatoes, corn and any other Jamaican type crops we could find and we walked to our neighbour's houses without being invited, just like we did in Jamaica. Though our little community grew in strength, it was still subject to the same kind of prejudices as other black communities. But we held fast, supporting each other, Caribbean people, African Americans and Native Americans.

Our little shop prospered but it was not long before my father's old itch flared up. He began telling duppy stories and jokes to anyone who came to the shop. Mama had to admit she enjoyed his stories; the man was very good at it. She even wanted to support his storytelling if only he would not, according to her, full my head with stupid, backward ideas about duppies and rolling calves. Moreover, she felt the shop was not the place to tell stories, especially since daddy always embarrassed her with his raw chaw Jamaican patois.

One busy Saturday, Daddy and a few friends gathered in one corner of the shop. He was the focus of attention telling one of his favorite duppy stories. My mother was as angry as a bear. She began shouting. "Lester, how can you stay there talking about duppy when the people need service."

Not moving, daddy said, "Gwaan serve dem Isabel, mi soon come."

Mama moved impatiently away from the counter to face him. "From now on Lester, you don't tell nuh more story in this shop. Or I am leaving!" She snapped, viciously.

Daddy realized she was not joking and immediately joined her in selling the shoppers. Later, he said, "You know Isabel, me faada used to tell duppy stories in Highgate. Fi 'im great, great grandfather before 'im was a storyteller in Africa - it in di family. How else di younger ones dem ago know dem history? Somebody must carry on di tradition, an' me have di gif'."

She laughed a little. "You really have the talent you know."

He shook his head. "Den mek me gwaan tell mi likkle story. Don't interfere wid me."

"Lester," she said earnestly, "back home we used to gather on the back-steps and tell stories. We used to enjoy the Anansi and Breddah Tacoomah stories and the whole lot of duppy stories you use to tell. But now the only kind of story you want to tell is about duppy. Duppy! Duppy! Duppy! Everything is duppy."

"But duppy and evil spirit deh."

"Yes, there is evil spirit and ghost too but why everything is duppy?"

"Me understand weh yuh a seh because my granpappy use to tell all kind a story," he paused. "But a nuff duppy deh a Highgate. An' people love fi hear 'bout dem." Daddy scratched his chin, deep in thought for a while and then an idea hit him like a bolt of lightening.

"Look Isabel, mek we invite people fi hear real Highgate duppy story a Saturday night time a wi yard. If it used to work a Jamaica, it can work here to. Den mi nuh have fi tell nuh story at di shop."

Mama looked at him for a long time. She really loved him and wanted him to be happy, just as he always tried to make her happy. Her greatest concern, however, was her children - me in particular. She did not want me to follow in my father's footsteps. Despite her reservations, she agreed but noted that it had to be confined to Saturdays. Mama averted her eyes momentarily, then jerked her attention to him, right index finger pointing and shaking vigorously within inches of his face, left hand akimbo in her usual style, "Alright Lester, alright, but one thing," she hesitated just long enough to allow him to appreciate the seriousness of her words, "English Lester. You must use the Queen's English every time you tell your story."

He was pleased she had accepted his suggestion but now he found himself on the griddle and squirmed. Daddy had his own reasons for not always using Standard English, especially in his everyday life. After all, he thought, Jamaica's native language is patois. He wondered how he could get his stories across effectively without using his beloved patois. He felt his stories would not ring true if they were told in Standard English. He grinned as the thought hit him. Of course, he would narrate his story in English but to lend authenticity he'd have to sound 'Jamaican' when he was quoting. He figured he would be effective if he narrated in English and quoted the characters in patois.

"Isabel I agree wid yuh. I will tell di stories in English but a will have to use patois in some part."

"Why? Which part Lester?"

"Ok, dis is how mi plan fi do it. Me we talk di story -in English mind yuh but when mi a tell weh di people dem seh, mi a go talk jus' like di people dem talk -in patois."

Mama did not give herself enough time to understand what daddy was explaining and objected immediately. "No sir. It not necessary," she said skeptically.

"Isabel -mi story a go come in like it not true; like it false if mi mek Jamaican people dem talk like English people. Dem have fi sound Jamaican."

After she thought about it, an understanding dawned on her. "Yuh right Lester, yuh right. Ok, gwaan tell your story like you just explain. I think it will be good."

Daddy laughed and gave her a friendly squint. Now he could really get into his storytelling quoting in patois while narrating in Mom's preferred language. His spirit soared as he realized the stories could now satisfy a larger audience than Jamaicans, as Native Americans and African Americans would now understand his stories. Mama was very happy with his promise and they parted thrilled with each other.

Saturday night came and we gathered in a semicircle on our veranda stairs to listen to father tell his stories. He sat on the upper stair looking down at us seated on the ground - just as we use to do in Jamaica. Initially, daddy forgot his promise to mama but a look from her quickly cured any amnesia that he may have had. He immediately switched to Standard English surprising many who knew him. What they didn't know was that my father was one of Highgate primary school's best English students. Daddy told us that in his school days his teachers were very strict about children learning the rules of concord and grammar and often used the whip to ensure they learnt well. He had attended school up to sixth class and was quite proficient, even in English Literature. We all guessed he had his secret reasons for not wanting to use Standard English regularly, a secret, we hoped, he would someday explain. From that night, daddy spoke fluently and only used patois for drama whenever he told one of his stories.

Attendance at our first Saturday night storytelling was scanty. Present were mama; my sister, Pamela; mother's friend, Carmen; one of daddy's friends, Mass Joe; and me. We were all a little disappointed, but daddy still maintained his usual cheer and said, "A nuh same day leaf drop a water bottom it rotten."

Daddy told an old story we heard in Jamaica before but which was new to our friends. It was about an old man from Highgate who died falling down his front door steps. For months after, the old man's duppy haunted the house. The local obeah men and Pocomania preachers could not get rid of the duppy. It was only after a well-known obeah man came all the way from St. Thomas and worked his magic that the duppy disappeared, never to be seen again. Of course, daddy made the story much creepier than we had heard it though it was substantially a more funny story than a scary one.

The word spread about our Saturday night storytelling, inveigling many from our neighbourhood to invite themselves. Daddy scheduled the next storytelling for two weeks time. I was brimming with excitement when I saw the number of people who came. They included the Bensons who used to live next door (Sheila, Terry, Joseph and their mother); Hopi and Mojoe, my two Native American friends; and Perry the local meat man. It was so successful that daddy wanted to hold a storytelling Saturday night on a regular basis. He suggested we do so maybe every other Saturday night but Mama wouldn't have any of it, agreeing to one every first Saturday in the month.

Those storytelling Saturday nights grew to represent chilling times in our lives and we enjoyed them tremendously. I got so caught up, to the delight of my father and the dismay of my mother, that I looked forward to these nights more than anything else. I remember the Saturday night of June 2nd 1951. The night was cool and we sat in a semi circle, daddy on the stairs facing us and mama sitting with my sister, Pamela and me. Daddy leaned backward in his chair and stretched. He had a twinkle in his eyes.

"I don't know if dis is a good night to tell yuh about 'Ayite, the slave girl'," he said with a frown. "Why not?" asked Hopi.

"Because yuh can neva be certain deze Duppy dem not around. Is nights like dis dem come looking fo' trouble. Especially when dem hear dem name call."

We all looked at each other, a spooky feeling creeping through the group.

"Anyway," he continued, "might jus' as well tell it, 'cause I don't want to go to di grave wid it."

And so, he began to tell us the story of Kavirondo and Ayite. Daddy's most polished voice resounded in the evening wind as he began. "Long, long ago," he said, "there was a big black man named Kavirondo..." It was on these lines that we became unfathomably lost in the depth of Daddy's entwining story.

Ayite, the Slave Girl

Kavirondo squeezed through the open window. The living room was pitch dark and the climb over the verandah rail forced him to breathe heavily. He did not expect to find a living soul awake at this time of night, they would have all been sleeping on the other side of the building; nevertheless he was cautious. He stood silently for a while, only the white of his dancing eyes visible in the dark. The July tropical heat of Highgate caused the sweat to break on his brows and roll down his face in streams. The man's two hundred and ten pounds coerced a squeak from the polished cedar floor as he tiptoed towards the fuzzy lamplight streaking under the big wooden door of the study.

The banana worker grew more confident once he entered the dimly lit study and found it empty. He approached the desk and, just as he was about to open the drawer, he noticed the piece of paper; it was a bill of sale. Kavirondo recognized it immediately; after all he had seen his - twice - before he became a free man.

"Free man," he mumbled shaking his head, "emancipation, yea, emancipation they called it." His eyes stared at the date on the paper: June 10th 1840. Lifting the document and looking closely at it he read:

> *June 10th 1840: Claire Benoist, to John Bresac, Bill of Sale for a slave named Ayite from the Accra People of The Gold Coast, about 25 years of age.*

His heart began to thump ominously against his chest.

"So Massa John still a buy slave though it illegal. All di more reason fi tek 'im money," he whispered noiselessly.

Kavirondo carefully replaced the bill of sale and opened the drawer. Two neat stacks of English Pounds rested in the left hand corner and smaller bills and coins were strewn all over the drawer. He took both stacks and stuffed a handful of smaller bills in his pocket. Ignoring the coins and remaining bills, he moved like a shadow, through the room, out the window and into the darkness.

Baku always slept in the shed next to the big house whenever Mass Peter stayed with his mother in their one-room barrack. The stubby retarded sixteen-year-old was awakened by the sound of urgent footsteps approaching his shed. He darted to his feet, powerful legs carrying him like a cat to the bamboo door. His heart pounded as he squeezed his shaggy eyebrows to the holes in the wickerwork, rolling his eyeballs as they tried to pierce the darkness.

The retard trembled in anticipation as fearful thoughts raced through his mind. Over a year now, Bully, the wickedest, most feared butcher, in St. Mary died. Since then, many people had seen his duppy. Some say Bully turned into the most dangerous rolling calf, with flaming eyes and a long chain trailing behind him. Tilley, his mother, told him never try to touch the chain of a rolling calf because the duppy will turn and rip his heart out. She said the only way to escape a rolling calf is to stick a knife in the ground and run without looking back. Once your back is turned, the duppy can't go any further; it must stop.

The young lad, shaking like a leaf and, anticipating the sight of the terrible rolling calf, was relieved to see Kavirondo running doggedly away from the big house towards the shed. Then, he saw her, a dark, slender woman dressed in full white trailing the big man.

The woman was captivating; tall and well-shaped, dress flowing to the ground covering her feet. He couldn't tell if she was running or floating. A cool breeze whisked through the shed causing the boy to shiver, as the woman passed. She turned, looked directly at him, smiled and disappeared into the darkness.

Baku was terrified. He knew Kavirondo was coming from the big house and at this time of night it could only mean the man was up to no good. Why was he coming from the big house? Did he go there to steal something? He would certainly get in trouble and Busha would certainly skin him alive. And, who was this woman he had never seen before? Could she be for real? No! No! She must be a ghost. He wanted to run home and tell his mother, but Tilley would be angry if he went there while Mass Peter was visiting. The boy did not get a drop of sleep until the wee hours of the morning.

In the meantime, Kavirondo reached his room without incident. He quickly dug up the flooring and hid the money in a hole, in the ground, he had prepared. Carefully, he replaced the loose floorboard, dusted them off so that they looked undisturbed and went to sleep. His head hardly touched the pillow when he had a strange dream. He dreamt he had gone to join his friends down by the bamboo building. Everyone from the barracks were there talking and having a good time. On his approach, they all stopped, turned and stared at him accusingly.

"Why unno a look pan mi fo'?" He asked, taken aback. No one answered; they just stared with the same unsettled look on all their faces. Kavirondo approached, hands outstretched, palms turned upward.

"What me do?" he pleaded, "Wha' wrong?"

The silence was bitter and thick, hanging like a cloud over the group. The disturbed Kavirondo wished he could fade away, just disappear, and then she stepped forward; a tall, slim black girl he had never seen before. Her appearance was so striking that everyone around her faded in the distance, leaving her standing there as rigid as the oak, head held high, accusing eyes shooting fire at his very being.

He stepped back subconsciously.

"Why yuh 'ere Kavirondo?" she asked.

"Who is yuh? An' 'ow yuh know mi name?" He heard himself asking.

"What yuh want here?" she shot back forcibly.

He stood there appalled, unable to comprehend what was happening.

"Nutten, nothing," he said simply.

"Well go! GO!"

"Why? What me do wrong?" he pleaded, looking at her outstretched hand pointing in the direction from whence he came.

"We nuh need yuh here."

"Why?"

"We nuh like t'ief and yuh a t'ief."

He looked at her and understood; they knew, yes, they all knew he had stolen Busha's money. But Kavirondo had no plans to ever admit to stealing anything.

"'Ey," he began, "a who yuh a call t'ief?..." But the woman was changing before his very eyes. A moment ago, the most beautiful female he had ever seen stood before him. Now, she was replaced by the most heinous, foul smelling witch he could ever conceive. The demon laughed. It sent shivers down his spine. She was moving towards him in as if to rip out his eyes -he stood transfixed. As her talons swept towards his face, he awoke the sound of chilling laughter still ringing in his ears.

Highgate, St. Mary had the propensity for mellow summer mornings, of crystal clear dewdrops, of baking hot noontimes and tranquil evenings. This morning was typical. The early morning sleep refreshed Baku and he woke with a slow, twisted smile spreading across his thick lips. He stretched and immediately remembered the events of a few hours past. The lad made a decision then; he would try to forget everything about last night. Going through the door, he marched into the sunshine a happy though feeble-minded young boy.

Ayite arrived in the island of Jamaica one year to date. Her grandfather and two others from her village had died in the terrible journey they call 'The Middle Passage'. Slavery was abolished in Jamaica over a year by then, but greedy, illegal slavers still pillaged villages of Africa taking their ill-gotten cargo to the Caribbean and the Americas. On this scorching Monday, Ayite began cleaning Claire Benoist's bedroom as soon as the lady awoke. The room was hot, but a soft wind entered whizzing across her puzzled face. It rushed from one side of the room to the next, always lingering over her head. Suddenly, reality struck; it was her dead grandfather. She hit the floor hands first, her eyes closed and she fell in a trance. Ayite's head swam gently at first, then violently, shaking her body like a headless chicken. She saw it clearly, the Ankobra River where she loved to swim as a child. She saw the swan in the water, its face disfigured and puffy where the stone had struck, one wing broken, causing it to struggle to stay afloat. She tried to save the little bird but strong hands held her. She saw the powerful hands around her waist, but when she turned to face him, her adversary vanished.

As quickly as it happened, the moment passed and she was back in the room. Ayite stood up. Yes, she knew the future held problems for her and someone else, someone she would meet very soon. The young woman was certain she had to save the disfigured little swan someday. "Miisumo bo Ataa, Oyiwala don,"[1] she whispered in Ga, her native language.

That same day two members of the Day Guard, a branch of the Jamaica Militia, came to investigate the break-in of John and Elvira Bresac's house. The couple had called the Governor in Port Maria for help reporting the loss of over five hundred pound sterling, money they planned to take on their trip to England. The two military officers took a statement from the Bresacs. Normally, John Bresac would have dealt with the matter himself, finding the culprit, and ordering a flogging of at least twenty lashes, but the couple had to leave for Kingston to buy supplies and pick up a black girl who, they say, would replace big, fat, pregnant Tilley as the house help. Tilley could scarcely move and was no longer doing a satisfactory job. Everyone liked Tilley though, and did not want some unknown stranger replacing her in the big house. Tilley helped everyone with food and other stolen goods from the big house. Yes siree, they all liked Tilley. But rumor had it; Massa John employed a young girl from Kingston last month and it was she he was picking up today.

After the Bresacs left, the two Day-Guards dressed in their black hats, blue frocks, blue coats, and blue trousers, went to the barracks to further their investigations. No one, including Kavirondo, had any idea of who had done such a wicked act. Then one of the Militiamen, Private Bellinton, saw Baku skulking around the corner of the house.

"Come here boy," he ordered.

"Me sah?"

"Yes! You."

"Me neva see nothing sah."

"Are you certain you didn't steal the money."

"No sah, is nat me sah." Frightened now, he looked at Kavirondo. The investigator followed the boy's eyes as it came to rest on Kavirondo.

"Come here boy, come."

Arms around the lad's shoulder, Private Bellinton led him away from the crowd, and then turned sternly to Baku.

---

[1] Meaning: "I love you grandfather. Thank you."

"Now boy, tell me what you know or…"for emphasis he stared menacingly at the boy, "or I will lock you up."

Baku looked down at the shiny black boots of his interrogator, and then up at his steely eyes. His stare was as frightening as that of an angry white man.

"Ah nuh me sah, ah, ah Kavirondo."

"Yes Baku, go on."

"Las' night me a sleep when me hear something a lick 'gains' di bush dem. Me t'ink is di rollin' calf. When mi look, mi see Kavirondo a run from di big house. 'Im run right pass di shed and dash inna him house." Baku paused, not sure the investigator believed him.

"Go on boy, go on."

"Me nuh see nutten more sah. After dat, mi go sleep."

"Where did he hide the money, boy? Come now. Talk up man"

"Me nuh know sah." The boy paused. Then, as if a sudden thought hit him he pointed to Kavirondo's quarters.

" 'Im might a hide it in a 'im room unda di bed sah."

For the first time, the Englishman's eyes softened. The boy was right, he was going to find the money, but even if they did not, this boy was all the evidence he needed to send that thieving Kavirondo to jail. They both marched back to the crowd, now getting bigger. Kavirondo saw them coming - both staring directly at him. He felt apprehensive, but held his ground.

"Kavirondo! Baku told me he saw you coming from Mr. Bresac's house last night. He was in the shed an' saw everything."

Kavirondo could not believe his ears. He looked around, shifty eyes glaring at Baku, ready to flee but Sergeant Rollins' gun was already drawn, leveled straight at his chest. Kavirondo impulsively raised his hands - chest high, fingers pointing outwards in surrender.

"It wasn't me sah," he pleaded, shaking his handsome head vigorously.

"Ok let's take a look in your house."

"Yes sah, come mek mi show yuh. Is not me sah."

The two Englishmen tore the place apart but failed to find the money. Sergeant Rollins was a bit skeptical, but Bellinton assured him, Kavirondo was the culprit. Together, they questioned Baku again. The boy held to his words making a convincing evidence against Kavirondo.

"You are going to prison Kavirondo," spat Bellinton, clearly disappointed he did not find the money, "but for your own good, tell us where you hid the money."

"Money sah? A nuh me sah."

"We'll ask Mr. Bresac to take it easy on you if you return the money," he cajoled.

"But a nuh me sah. Please Massa, 'elp me nuh."

"We know it's you boy."

But Kavirondo stuck to his guns and kept his story straight.

They moved out then, the Militiamen, Baku, Kavirondo and a crowd in tow, up the road to Highgate town, to the little white building use as a holding cell for criminal waiting to be shipped to the Port Maria Jail. Word traveled fast, as big, fat James Lickly, the ex-slave who attended the place whenever a prisoner checked in, was waiting.

"Yuh done get yuh self inna trouble now eh Kavirondo?"

"Mi nuh do nutten Lickylicky," wailed Kavirondo using James Lickly's nickname.

"Den why dem a go lock yuh up?"

"A Baku tell lie pan me. Help mi nuh Lickylicky."

"Cyaan 'elp yuh bwoy, till yuh confess an' show dem weh di money deh."

Kavirondo fell silent.

Once inside, the officers questioned Baku rigorously, making notes and taking a formal statement, yet he never said a word about the woman he saw following Kavirondo.

Kavirondo sat quietly and when Baku was finished Rollins turned to him.

"Why did you steal the money boy?"

"A lie 'im a tell sah."

"You were never at the house that night?"

"No sah. Mi neva leave mi house de whole night."

"Shut up liar."

"A true mi a tell sah."

The Englishmen jailed Kavirondo, charging him for the theft of five hundred pounds twelve shillings, the property of John Bresac. For two days, he stayed in the holding cell getting one meal per day. The third day, he was released and ordered to appear in the Port Maria Court of Petty Sessions in two months.

Sergeant Rollins did not particularly like Baku, but he was the only witness, and with him they might be able to squeeze a confession from the big ex-slave and retrieve the money. They promised to transport Baku to the Port Maria courthouse, seven miles away from Highgate, while Kavirondo had to find his own way there.

Eight o'clock Friday morning, four days after leaving their home, John Bresac's carriage rolled through the large Iron Gate. Both horses were tired, the grueling journey from Kingston taking its toll. A cart with supplies and a large bundle covered with a blanket was hitched to the carriage. Tom pulled the carriage to a stop before the big house.

"We is reach Busha."

"Uh huh," came the gruffly voice of John Bresac. Stepping from the carriage, he lifted his wife to the ground and went to unhitch the cart.

"Wake up girl," he prodded the blanket-covered bundle. Suddenly, it came alive as Ayite pushed the covers away and sat upright. She hissed at him and jumped to her feet. Bresac caught her by the waist and held her firmly. It was then everyone noticed she was tied loosely to cart.

"You are home now girl," John Bresac said firmly. She stared defiantly without speaking. He pulled her closely and unhitched the rope. Ayite stared cheekily at the crowd; beautifully strong legs anchoring her five foot ten body firmly to the ground. Majestic and proud, head held high, she slowly appraised her surroundings. Though she did not show it, these strange people frightened her. *They were all Africans*, she thought, *but they have come to love this land.* She wanted desperately to go home, to be with her people, her family and her friends.

Kavirondo saw her when he came around the corner. Never before had he seen an African woman with such stately bearing. She looked like a queen and very familiar. The big man pulled his eyes away surveying the area, trying to locate John Bresac whom he had come to see. He must convince Busha he did not steal the money. He knew John Bresac well, the white man would beat him to death; twenty or more lashes if he ever proved he Kavirondo stole the money. There was no turning back now. He must convince them Baku was lying. If he could find a way to put some of the money in the shed, they would believe Baku gave away the money and hid the rest there. After all, Baku was not 'righted' and it was easy to believe he did it. He saw John Bresac standing beside the girl, but he could not tear his eyes away from her. As he looked at her, a tight uneasy feeling began in his toes, crept up his spine, pervading his entire body. Something about this imposing stranger caused him to be afraid.

Ayite saw him coming, her eyes narrowed in a dead stare. The mighty

Kavirondo stopped in his tracks and shivered. It was she; it was the woman in his dreams, the same one who had turned into the hideous witch. A bizarre premonition of his doom spread over his entire being.

"Come girl! Stay in the Barrack with Tilley until John has your room ready," Elvira Bresac said holding on to Ayite's elbow. The girl pulled away but moved in the direction she was guided.

"Tom! Walk with this girl over to Tilley house fi mi nuh."

"Yes Mam."

The old man and girl walked around the house towards the housing area while the bystanders dispersed.

Tilley was angry, not only was she about to lose her job to this stranger, she had to accommodate her, allowing her to stay in her room -no more privacy. Well! She will have to sleep on the ground. She met Ayite at the door with a cold stare. Ayite stared back with a smile and Tilley immediately knew it; this woman was different. She felt something she had never felt before and was forewarned. Yes! There was something powerful about this majestic young girl that would make her a better friend than an enemy.

They sat on the bed edge and chatted for a while, and then Baku walked in. He stopped abruptly and stared. For a moment, he could utter no words while his trembling hands pointed at Ayite, fear twisted his already distorted face.

"Ah, ah yuh mi see ah, ah, follow Kavirondo las' night," he stammered.

"What? Yuh fool-fool bwoy?" Tilley barked.

"No Mam, mi see har..."

Tilley looked at Ayite then back to her son: "Yuh a dream bwoy, she jus' come dis mornin'."

Ayite smiled and stepped towards Baku, she wore the same knowing smile of last night. Unexpectedly, the fear disappeared and he felt a deep sense of calm and amity. She held his hands and for the first time spoke.

"Mi jus' come," she said simply.

From that minute on, they both liked each other, the beautiful ex-slave girl and the sixteen year-old. Suddenly, it dawned on Ayite. *This is my little swan.*

Kavirondo was disturbed to say the least. Mr. Bresac did not believe he was innocent and threatened to skin him alive, jail him and then throw away the key. He had to do something to save himself and it did not include returning the money. Never! He couldn't give it back. He thought of running away, but where could he go? He was born and bred in Harmony Hall; the furthest he had ever traveled was to Port Maria. He was afraid, running away was not the answer because they would find him plus he couldn't live in the bushes alone with all those duppies and rolling calves.

He thought of blackmailing John Bresac, he had proof the man was still dealing in the slave trade, but he realized the authorities would never believe a black man against the powerful Busha and he would certainly be killed. He was now sorry that he did not keep the bill of sale. He shook his head in desperation. What the hell could he do to save himself? Well! There was only one thing for him to do, much as he hated the thought. He had to do it.

Kavirondo did not know the Bresacs paid for Ayite because they could not find good help in the district and blacks in Kingston did not want to work in the country. Ayite was free the moment she left the Benoists. They told her she would receive regular wages, same as they paid Tilley. True, she was frightened and did not want to leave; they had to forcibly take her. John Bresac wanted her to see her new house and to experience working for them. Then, if she still wanted to go, they would release her.

Both John and Elvira liked her and, despite the tales they heard, they were not afraid of her alleged powers. They knew her background very well. They knew she was the daughter of a Klote Lagoon, the keeper of the oral traditions, the interpreter of the gods, who is said to know all things present and in the future. But they decided, long ago, she was the perfect help they needed.

The Bresacs were correct; Ayite soon began to like her surroundings. People in the area liked her but thought that she was very strange. She loved animals and took over Tom's job of tying out the horses and donkey at nights. People said she spoke their language, because they always understood her and seemed to be telling her things. How else could she know some of the things she knew?

One day her little swan told her he was afraid of Kavirondo.

"Why little one?" she inquired.

"'Cause him hates me."

"Because yuh tell di police yuh see him run from de house afta him t'ief di money?

Baku was shocked, how did she know that?

"Don't worry Baku, me know say a him to."

" 'Im tell mi fi seh a lie mi was telling."

"Yuh a go do dat?"

"No! Mi tell him no and him say him will kill me if me go a court"

"Yuh do di right t'ing Baku. Don't worry, di police will protect yuh."

"But me fraid a him - Ayite."

"Hush Baku. Him not going do yuh nothing."

The boy walked away. She was concerned. Would she be able to protect her little swan?

Two nights later Baku did not come home. They all thought he was sleeping in the shed close to the big house, but he did not turn up the next day or the next. Ayite knew something bad befallen her swan but Tilley and the other workers believed he had run away fearing Kavirondo would hurt him.

On the third night, Ayite was tying out the donkey when he stopped and would not budge.

"Come Adrian," she cajoled.

The donkey wouldn't move, its eyes flamed, turning blazing red, it snorted, froth flying from its mouth. She stepped back: "La,"[2] she shouted, reverting to her native tongue.

The donkey reared and dashed towards the trail leading to the river. Ayite jumped on its back; together they raced towards Jimmy River.

"Neegbe oyaa? Neegbe oyaa?[3]" She kept asking, as they raced wildly down the hill.

It was dusk by the time they entered the river stream, Ayite was certain now the donkey was taking her to Baku. Then it stopped abruptly, throwing her to the ground. She rolled and stopped by a clump of bushes where Baku's bloody body lay, a knife protruding from his throat. His unseeing eyes stared up at her.

For the first time since embarking from the terrible ship, she cried. When she was finished, she remounted the donkey and rode directly to the big house. Ayite felt she had failed her little swan and her only comfort was knowing he had returned to Africa.

During the days following Baku's death, there was great lamentation,

---

[2] Means: "fire" in Ga.
[3] "Where are you going?"

mourning and howling. Everyone in Highgate knew Kavirondo had gone and killed him, but no one could prove it and the big man denied even seeing the boy.

The funeral was arranged for the coming Sunday and as was customary the dancing, beating of drums and mournful singing began. Then, early that Sunday morning, Ayite called Tilley and a few others together and told them she was going to get Baku's murderer; she outlined her plan. She explained that in her village, the spirit of the dead communicated with them and revealed their killers. She promised to talk to Baku.

"We must give Baku the chance to tell us who killed him," she explained

"Mi poor boy," wailed Tilley.

"Lead di way," said Tom.

That Sunday afternoon, they placed Baku's coffin in the open field behind the big house and prayed. He was to be buried down the gully where workers from the estate barracks were buried. Ayite led the march from the house to the gully burial ground carrying a white flag. Four men carried the coffin, two at the head and two at the foot. The men easily sling the brown wooden coffin on two pieces of rope on either end.

Halfway there, Ayite shouted, "Stop!"

She placed her ears in a listening attitude against the coffin. Then she declared to every one, "Baku, him angry." She listened again, "Baku want unno to stop at 'im modda yard," she paused dramatically, "him will tell wi who kill him."

"Give wi a drink," shouted one of the pallbearers. Immediately, they were presented with renewed portions of rum. Kavirondo, mingling in the crowd, was getting more fearful by the minute but determined not to show it. Pretending he wanted to know who killed Baku also, he shouted:

"Yes Ayite we have to fin' out who kill likkle Baku."

"Move wid di coffin," shouted Ayite.

The pallbearers began their journey again, procession in tow, coffin jerking from side to side. Soon, they were at the barracks. Ayite beckoned the pallbearers to move forward. She placed her ears beside the coffin.

"Baku! Baku! Tell mi a who do it."

She listened and shook her head.

"'Im want Kavirondo fi 'elp carry di coffin."

Kavirondo stepped forward and courageously took one end of the rope from the pallbearer at the head of the coffin, "Yes Ayite," he said bravely, "lead di way."

White flag in hand, Ayite led the procession towards the burial ground taking a path directly adjacent to Kavirondo's room. Singing and dancing, swaying the coffin from side to side the drunken crowd marched. Then, just as they reached Kavirondo's lodgings, the coffin jerked, Kavirondo pitched forward and the box fell heavily to the ground, rolling down the grade and resting at Kavirondo's doorsteps.

The silence was thick as rain clouds. Everyone stared at Kavirondo and he was petrified.

"Kavirondo," Ayite snarled, emotions building like wildfire in her breast, "Mi did know seh a yuh. Yuh done t'ief Busha money and den kill poor Baku."

"No! No! A lie," wailed Kavirondo, stepping back in mortal fear.

"Liar, thief, murderer," she spat, eyes flashing spears of hate.

"Mi vision yuh myself. Mi know it before Baku tell mi. A fi mi spirit did a follow yuh di night yuh t'ief di money."

The big man turned and ran towards the bushes.

"Gwaan! Kavirondo, but rememba evildoers can't escape retribution fi long," she shouted. They buried Baku and returned to their barracks.

The days passed and the case against Kavirondo was dropped for lack of proof. John Bresac called the whole coffin incident hocus pocus, and did not accept the story as proof of Kavirondo's guilt. But he secretly believed the big man committed the crime, so he allowed the people to deal with him according to their own customs. Much as he wanted his money back he could not in all honesty punish Kavirondo without proof. As such, he still allowed the ex-slave to work on his estate. Kavirondo's day-to-day punishment was awful; very few people even spoke to him and he became an outsider. One day, he walked close enough to Ayite and heard her singing in Ga:

Retribution a come soon
By fire, by water, or by brimstone
Yuh will pay de price

He shivered and hurried along his way. Three nights later Kavirondo heard the first stone fall on the roof of his room. He went outside to see who was throwing stones but there was no one in sight. Large stones kept pelting the side and top of the building but no one was ever seen throwing them. For the entire day, the stoning continued. Word spread and people gathered to witness stones falling from the sky. Fearful, Kavirondo begged Ayite to let them stop it but she just kept on singing.

The second night after the stones started Kavirondo saw a boy, who looked just like Baku, walking toward his house then disappeared in thin air. Soon, he realized he was being tormented regularly by Baku's duppy. Still, the big man kept quiet, refusing to admit any wrongdoing. Then, stones began hitting him directly. People say they see the stones hurtling through the air, and the bruises on his body; but they never saw who threw them. Many, many people, from Highgate followed the luckless Kavirondo around to see where the stones came from, but even to this day only Ayite knew.

One day, a stone made a huge gash on Kavirondo's head. For the first time, the big man cried. Soon, he began mumbling incoherently, the only recognizable words were 'Baku' and 'sorry'. He stopped eating and cleaning himself. That's when the people realized he had gone out of his mind.

To this day, those who know the story of Kavirondo wondered how he remained sane for so long. He wandered the streets lamenting and calling Baku's name for days before they found him dead at the steps of his house.

Ayite was contented; her little swan was safe back in Osu, where his spirit would roam free forever. She smiled, knowing she would lead the procession for Kavirondo, the white flag flying high at his burial.

Daddy ended his story with a sigh which sounded much like the release of gas from a pressure chamber. It was the only sound in the still of the night as I shivered, hot as it was, and everyone hugged themselves, looking starry-eyed. He smiled, satisfied at the effect of his story on the audience, stood up, and stretched.

"Well," he said, a broad satisfying smile on his face, "we should all go to bed now. No sense in providing company for them duppies hanging out around here." He was about to leave when Sheila Benson spoke.

"What happened to the money? No one ever found it?"

Daddy sat heavily with pretense weariness.

"Yes, years later. Long, long after Ayite and Tilley died..." his voice tailed away as if lost in memory.

"Tilley gave birth to a beautiful girl child - Bacora they call her, after her brother Baku. Well, she married one of Deacon Morrison's bwoys..."

"Who is Deacon Morrison?" I asked.

"That's another story my boy, for anodder time. Anyway, the couple saved and bought the piece of land with the barracks on it. Busha Bresac and his wife went back to England. They sold the house and land. It was not until after Bacora and her husband tore down the barracks that they found the money. The couple knew the entire story about Kavirondo and realized it must be the money Kavirondo stole and hid. They took the money to the authorities in Highgate, but after a while the authorities gave most of it back to them."

"What a lucky set of people," observed Carmen. "Sorry it wasn't me," she said with a snicker, showing authentic sorrow.

A murmur of agreement went up from the audience but daddy continued.

"They had the right to the money," he said, a sneer of self-righteousness sitting evenly on his face.

"Anyway, according to the authority the money belongs to the two married people because there was no one in Jamaica to make claim to it. Further, the Morrisons owned the land where the money was found. The couple used their money to build a beautiful little house on the same spot where the barracks were."

Daddy finished with a smile; once again he had held the interest of his entire audience. He believed he enjoyed telling his stories more than anyone enjoyed listening to them. My father went to bed content and I dozed with solemn thoughts of Jamaican duppies, obeah and murder, anticipating the stories to come at our next Saturday night storytelling. I also knew I wanted to become a storyteller like my daddy.

Chapter 2

I went to the market with my mother the Saturday of July 7th 1951, but I was dying for night to come as I looked forward to my father's stories more than anything else in my whole life. Mama must have noticed my anxiety because she immediately asked me how I was doing in school, a practice she had when she wanted to talk to me about getting good grades instead of focusing on storytelling. Mom followed my school-work keenly and knew whenever I wasn't doing well. There was no other reason for her to ask.

As soon as I became engrossed in daddy's storytelling, my grades began to suffer terribly. I didn't see the need for school, least of all to study hard, because I was going to become a storyteller.

"Cecil," she had said, "son look all around you. What do you see?"

"Don't know what yuh talking 'bout ma."

"Son, don't you see how things are here in America. White people, they are rich while black people - they are mostly poor? Son, it's not like Jamaica at all. Over here, white people treat blacks like they are still slaves. We can't even go into their restaurants. They have the best schools while most of us can barely afford food and we work for them. If it was-n't for the hard work your father and me put into the shop, we wouldn't even have money to come to the market. Do you want to turn out to be something or do you want to be like your father? Eh? Is that how you want to live for the rest of your life Cecil -eh?"

"No Ma," I responded nonchalantly.

"Son, storytelling can't help you. Study hard, pay attention in school, and one day you can become a doctor or a lawyer. You can make some-thing of your life."

"But Ma…" I barely protested.

"But nothing Cecil. Your father and me, one day we will be old and you will be taking care of yourself. You want to turn wutless and walk 'bout telling duppy story like yuh father?"

"Daddy isn't wutless, Ma," I shot back in defense of my father.

"I didn't say he was son. I said if you don't do well in school you'll be worthless. Your father's days and your days are different. You'll see son, you'll see."

I heard Ma and felt concerned but storytelling was exciting and I knew I'd do well at it. Nothing would ever stop me from becoming a great storyteller.

On our way home, we saw my two Native American friends who seemed as eager as me for the impending evening time when we could listen to daddy's duppy story. Their faces lit up when they saw us and anxiously asked Mom if their mother could join us for storytelling. Mama told them she was very welcome. We later learned Mrs. Kaneohe, Mojoe and Hopi's mother, came because the boys were afraid to walk home alone after hearing my father's stories. She did not want them to be a bother to daddy who would have gladly accompanied them anyway.

All three of them were present at our doorstep by twilight on that muggy Saturday. The falling of night did not ease the humidity as the heat hung like a blanket all around us and sweat oozed from our pores and ran like rivulets down our faces. We fidgeted as we sat waiting for Mama to bring the refreshments.

While we waited, Mojoe asked his mother to tell a Native American ghost story but Mrs. Kaneohe laughingly told him she wanted to hear our Jamaican stories and when the time was right she would ask her husband to invite us over for their own storytelling. Little did she know that they would be so caught up in daddy's storytelling that they would never get the chance to tell their own Native American stories.

The crowd was larger than last time as there were at least two persons present whom we did not know. We later learned that Gladys and Maryellen were friends of the Bensons. They had traveled from Fort Lauderdale to visit their friends and came over to hear daddy's story. We got to understand they were Jamaicans and knew of many cases of duppies appearing to people and, in some instances, even hurting people. They told us they personally know of an evil obeah man who actually controlled duppies. The only people who were protected from his evil deeds were those who always had good duppies walking with them.

It's funny how life is when one is engrossed in things they love; all discomforts disappeared when mama distributed the refreshing lemonade although Daddy wasn't ready to tell his story. Gladys and Maryellen did-n't mind because they were getting all our attention. Both girls were in their early teens and were enjoying the attention my two Native American friends, my sister and I were paying them. They told us a Jamaican duppy story, which I remember vividly. It was not so much about duppy as it was about obeah. Gladys began:

"Yuh see di wicked obeah man, who live a Highgate, dat we was telling yuh about?"

We all shook our heads with deep curiosity.

"Well, one day a woman came to 'im for help. She said dat her husban' always visit anodda 'oman down di road name Dorothy. When she talk to him, 'im jus' quarrel and push her away. If she keep talking, him beat her up."

"Eh-eh," responded Maryellen, showing a sad face and shaking her head up and down frighteningly.

"Di obeah man ask di 'oman what she want him fi do. Di 'oman say she don't know."

"Yuh want mi kill di bugga fi yuh?"

"No, no don't kill him!" Di 'oman start fi cry.

'Well, what yuh want den?"

"Henyting fi help mi sah. Me jus' want 'im fi stap go a road."

"Ok! Mi ago beat 'im backside fi yuh."

"Yes sah! Beat im an' tell im nuh fi go a road sah."

"Di obeah man charge' her a whole heap a' money an' tell her fi go home, everyt'ing well be aright." Gladys paused and looked at us.

"What happened?" Mojoe asked frightened and out of breath although he was sitting quietly.

Maryellen spoke up. "Di nex' day di man wake up a bawl. 'Im holla and holla jumping out of di bed. Di 'oman ask im, 'What wrong?' but him jus' a bawl and a bawl. Den him faint and fall down pan di floor. When di 'oman look pan him shirt back, it was soaking in blood. She tek off him shirt and a pure wail she see, as if someone tek a whip an' beat di hell out a 'im."

We were shocked, all of us, we just sat staring at the two girls. Then Maryellen continued.

"For three nights straight, the duppy dem beat di man, till 'im have to beg di 'oman fi help. She tell him seh dat a di 'oman him a visit down di

27

road put duppy pan him. She tell him say dat di 'oman do it so dat him will leave him good, good, married house. She tell im dat if him stop go a her yard, she personally will go to another obeah man and mek 'im tek care a di duppy dem.

"Di man believe her and beg her fi tek weh di duppy dem. Di 'oman go back to di obeah man and 'im charge her double di amount fi stop di duppy dem. She have fi go borrow di money fi pay 'im. Di beatin' stop an' her husban' neva go back a di odder woman yard again."

Needless to say, the story shook us to the bones. We were already terrified when Daddy began his story.

We hardly heard him at first, then his voice seeped into our heads, spiraling us to attention.

"When I was a boy," he began, "people in Highgate was not afraid of any outsiders. Their cutlass was their friend and they would use it in the blinking of an eye. Yep, Highgate people were renowned for their swift and deliberate use of the machete, often chopping off others head at the simplest provocation."

"If someone's head is severed, locals know they had to bury both head and body together. Sometimes murderers buried head separate from body causing big problems. Many a time, folks have seen headless duppies walking at nights looking for their heads. Some people swear they have seen a duppy head looking for the body. All kinds of things have happened in Highgate. But this story beats them all. It is about two sisters who lived in Highgate. As you know..."

Two Sisters For England

The parish of St. Mary, Jamaica, West Indies, is well known for its magnificent rolling hills, winding roads, tantalizing greenery and its warm friendly people, but no place on earth has had more bloody machete murders, more obeah men, or more encounters with the dead (the terrifying Duppy) than Highgate, St. Mary. And yet, not even the peaceful folks of this bucolic little town could have imagined the events that were to take place in the dingy two-bedroom house owned by Tom Francis.

Tom worked like a slave that day. He must have cut and carried sixty bunches of bananas, on his shoulder, from the plantation to the shipping station. And each bunch was at least seven hands. It was no wonder that locals considered him the strongest man on the plantation; the man could easily carry seven eight-hand 'bunch' of bananas at one time, strung all over his body. Francis reached home at precisely six o'clock that fateful Tuesday evening - his wife was waiting for him.

"Tom! Tom! De letta come." She said excitedly.

"Which letta?"

"Dis letta!" Her outstretched hands contained a blue overseas envelope. Tom, who couldn't read a word, made no attempt to take it.

"Whose letta?"

"It come from Mama."

Tom stared at her for a moment then briskly mounted the stairs, his massive frame bearing down mercilessly on the wooden steps. On the fourth flight, he sat heavily, the sun baked stair hollering in protest.

"What she have to seh?"

"Yuh nuh rememba Tom? A di invitation letta fi Cherry an' me! We have to show dem at de hembassy in Englan', to get in. An' she sen' di plane ticket dem to."

"Yuh an' Cherry alone?"

"Lawd Massa! We neva did discuss dis nuff time?"

"Tell me again man … tell me again."

"We agree seh, when me reach Englan', as soon as me get a job, me will

29

sen' fi yuh."

"Unno ago sen' fi me - eh?"

"But of course. Yuh know how Mama mean aready! She neva even want fi sen' de fare fi me an' Cherry. Yuh know she not goin' sen' no money fi yuh. De 'oman, meeeaaaan Tom … and yuh know it."

"A true dat," he said absentmindedly.

"But as soon as me work me own money, ah will send fi yuh."

"Uh! Uh! So, when unno goin'?"

"Next Sunday Tom," she answered somberly.

"So soon?"

She saw the fear in his pleading eyes and felt she had let him down - badly.

"Aaaah bwoy," he sighed, unno really goin' sen' fi mi?"

It was a question but he was shaking his head in disbelief, as if the question was already answered.

Doris felt his despair and knew she had to comfort him.

"Tom, yuh believe me would a go a Englan' an' nuh sen' fi you? Eh? Yuh mad? Of course mi a go sen' fi yuh."

Tom was silent for a moment. He believed his wife would keep her word but he was unsure of her other family especially, her sister Cherry. They hated him and wanted Doris to leave him. Just as he thought about Cherry, he saw her climbing the hill towards them; her pulling her two hundred and ninety pounds, up the hill, three steps at a time. She made a long moaning pause and rested after every three steps. As she ascended, her breathing got heavier and heavier and she prayed silently.

"Lawd Jesas, help me."

Tom smiled as he watched her. He was secretly hoping she would drop dead before reaching the house. Francis looked at his wife and wondered how such a simple, such a nice woman could have this kind of person, this ugly mammoth for a sister.

"Jacket," he whispered under his breath.

"What yuh seh Tom?" his wife asked.

"Nutten! Nutten man. Mi only hope dem mek yuh sen' fo' me"

Doris, whose back was to the road, turned and saw her sister. Excitedly, she started waving the letter.

"Cherry! Cherry! De ticket dem come!"

"T'ank yuh Lawd, t'ank yuh." Cherry responded, trying to move faster so she could retrieve the letter her sister was excitedly waving.

Breathing like a mule, she finally caught up to her sister and grabbed the letter. No one would believe Cherry was the younger sister. At age twenty-eight, she ate far too much and she was lazy.

"A can't wait till nex' Sunday," she said with abject glee.

But Doris had lost her excitement; she really felt sorry for Tom. He looked at them both, wanting his wife to stay as much as he wanted her sister to leave. He missed Doris already, this healthy, five foot nine, one-hundred-and-fifty-pound black woman. He loved her shapely figure, her full breasts and easy gait. Most men in Highgate believed she was a fine woman, with her dark chocolate skin and short jet-black hair. Some say her backside was too large, but Tom liked it very much - thank you.

Cherry finished reading the letter and smiled. She looked at Tom and jeered:

"Tom! A yuh alone a go stay in di house when wi gone. Don't carry any 'oman in here, yuh hear? Or we not goin' sen' fi yuh."

Tom stared balefully at her, refusing to give her the pleasure of a reply. He hated the big fat slob. Again, he looked at his wife; a slow smile crept across his face. She was the much, much better choice. Doris was not only more beautiful, but kinder and gentler. He knew he loved her though he sometimes got angry and beat her, but she loved him too because she always forgave him. Then, he hung his head as heaviness crept across his heart. One day, she would get her revenge for all those beatings though, but for now he wanted nothing more than to have her with him. The heaviness weighed tons at the thought of her leaving for England. That troublemaking sister Cherry and her mother was intent on taking her away from him and there was nothing he could do to stop them. Sadly, he heaved his big tired frame from the steps and walked unhurriedly towards the back of the two-bedroom house.

The two sisters watched him go, passing the outdoor kitchen, moving along the path towards the little latrine built from raw lumber and a few sheets of old zinc. They saw when he stopped at the side of the toilet and urinated, but they did not see when he turned back and entered the kitchen, where the big black yabba pot sat, filled to the brim with gungo peas soup. He was about to help himself when he heard them.

"What yuh mean yuh feel bad fi leave 'im? Look how much time 'im beat yuh! Yuh nuh tired to mek de ol' crufty man beat yuh up?

"Yes, but 'im don't really mean it yuh know Cherry. 'Im only get out of control when 'im drunk."

"Yuh a fool Doris? As soon as yuh gone, 'im a move one a dem nasty gal in a di house. Yuh t'ink him care. Once him have a woman, him won't even think 'bout yuh."

"A true. A rememba de odda day when mi catch him and de dutty gal Sonia in a de house. But bwoy mi feel bad to leave him here alone. We have to send fi him Cherry. But when him come him have to fend fi him-self."

"No! Doris no! Yuh don't hear What Mama seh? She don't want him up dere. She don't want him a Englan'. Leave him Doris, leave him h'out here. Plenty good man deh a Englan'."

"It hard fi do dat Cherry. It hard bad. Me an' Tom a come a long way."

"Doris? Me nah leave yah wid yuh, if yuh ago sen' fi dat man. Me a go write an' tell Mama why. Me an' yuh, an' 'im, nah go a Englan'."

"But Cherry…"

"No sah, ova mi dead bady."

"Ok Cherry! Ahrite! Ahrite! But yuh cyaan stop me from write 'im. Terrible as 'im is, 'im a still me 'usban'."

"Well a fi yuh business dat," retorted Cherry, glad her sister had decided to leave Tom. She was certain Doris would forget him once she reached England. She swaggered out of the room and slumped in the deep wooden chair Tom Francis made.

Tom was in a quandary. His heart started beating faster and faster at the thought of his beloved Doris leaving him forever. He couldn't bear the thought and certainly couldn't let that happen. He looked at the far corner of the kitchen and saw the cutlass where he had placed it between the wall and the post. Suddenly, he was certain of what he had to do. His blood began to boil as anger surged in his chest. He grabbed the machete and run his fingers across the blade. It was sharp, but he pulled the file from his waist and gave it a few strokes just to make sure it was sharp enough.

He ran from the kitchen to the veranda where Cherry was sitting. She saw him and knew; the mad look in his eyes told her everything. She screamed.

"No Tom! No…" but the blade shut off any further sound as it sunk deep in her fat neck like a hot knife through butter. She fell to the floor with a loud thud, blood gushing from her neck. Again, she tried to scream but only a gargling sound erupted from her blood filled mouth. Tom saw she was still alive; he seized her hair and twisted her neck in a grotesque way. The machete made a deadly arc and her head came away from her body in his hand. Immediately, he opened his hand and it fell to the wooden floor, making a muffled sound, flesh and blood spluttering on impact, just as Doris came to the door. Tom lunged at her, she turned and ran but the machete sliced through the air once more, making a deep gash across her bottom. She screamed and begged, but Tom was out of his mind with rage. He finished the job with a powerful swing to her head.

Francis looked around; there was no one in sight. He dragged Cherry's body and head into the house where his wife had fallen. For the next ten minutes, he sat beside his wife hugging her and crying. The murderer sank his nose in her warm neck and smelt the delicate scent of Jasmine, her favorite perfume.

"Yuh shouldn' follow yuh sista!" He wailed.

"Look how much mi love yuh Doris? Doris! Doris!"

Tom Francis cried until he lost track of time. So deep was his sadness that, at first, he contemplated killing himself, but depression turned to rage when he looked at Cherry's severed head and he felt a deep satisfaction in his gut. He felt no pity for her. Only disgust.

The night was cool and dark. Tom Francis waited until nearly eleven that night to bury the bodies. He dug nine holes behind the latrine where he placed Cherry, piece by piece into each of the eight holes. He wanted to make a regular grave for Doris but they would discover it, so he placed her body deep in a single hole and covered the graves with rows of vegetable beds. There, he planted carrots, peas, and cabbage and a few other vegetables.

The big man went back to the house and splashed buckets after buckets of water on the floor and scrubbed until he was satisfied there was no trace of blood anywhere. He was not finished until four o'clock that morning.

The days went by and the residents of Highgate began to ask for the sisters. Tom went about his business as usual carrying banana from the field to the shipping station, explaining that the sisters had gone to England and would soon be sending for him. He went to the post office and collected two letters from his wife's mother. He tore them up and dumped them. As the weeks passed, he changed his story saying his wife had betrayed him and would not be sending for him again. They were happy in England and had forgotten all about him. Soon he moved Marva, an old girlfriend, into the house. No one cared since Doris and her sister had deserted the poor man.

Early one morning, about four o'clock, Barry Millings decided to drive his old Oxford Cambridge to the City. The forty-year-old bachelor was new to Highgate and had recently bought a small grocery shop. His plans were to shop in Kingston for goods once per month; today was his first shopping trip. The shop owner had never met Tom Francis, his wife Doris, or her sister Cherry. On this chilly Monday morning, the Oxford Cambridge rumbled towards Tom Francis's house when, there before him, Barry saw two women, dressed in beautiful white clothes, thumbing a ride. One was very fat, while the other was nicely built.

He ran his hands across his graying beard in an attempt to groom it and thanked God he had shaved his head bald. A low chuckle escaped his lips as he mentally reviewed his last look in the mirror before leaving that morning. Black all the way: black shirt neatly tucked in his expensive black pants, with cuffs just touching his flashy black shoe, giving a glimpse of the black cotton socks. Yep! He smiled bringing the Oxford to a complete stop beside the hitchhikers.

"Jump in," he said, "I'm heading for Kingston."

The ladies smiled and moved towards the vehicle. He opened a back and a front passenger door. Ignoring the opened front door, they both climbed in the back. He shrugged and sped off for Kingston.

As he drove, Barry noticed an unusual chill in the air and the faint smell of Jasmine. He looked through the rear view mirror, his eyes focusing on the prettier lady, who looked at him shyly, a sweet, alluring smile spreading across her thick, dark lips, eyes ablaze with excitement. He sought conversation.

"Yuh live in that house where I picked you up?" He noticed them shaking their heads in the affirmative.

"What's your name?" Neither of them answered.

"Are you girls going to a wedding?" They giggled and shook their heads.

Barry soon realized the ladies were perfectly happy to indulge in a one-way conversation. His questions were met with giggles and happy nods, but no words were spoken. Soon, he felt tired of talking and drove quietly in to the big city.

At five thirty, he pulled up across from the imposing Carib Theatre in Cross Roads.

"This is as far as I go ladies. It's still a little dark but you can get a bus over there."

He leaned over and opened the door pointing to the bus stop adjacent to the car. As he leaned over, the stench was overpowering. He thought one of them must have passed some gas. He continued:

"Can I see you at the house when we get back to Highgate?"

Once again, there was vigorous nodding and sweet giggles but no words were spoken. Easily, they alighted from the car and they surprised him with the smoothness of their movement - especially the fat one. It was if they were floating out of the car.

"Ok!" He smiled, "Si yuh soon."

As he drove off he looked through the rear view mirror to see where they were going but they were nowhere to be seen. The only memory of their presence was the faint smell of Jasmine hanging in the air.

"Funny!" He whispered to himself but soon forgot about them as he went about his business.

That evening, after returning to his grocery store, Barry began inquiring about the two ladies living down the road but no one seemed to know them. Then, George Thompson got curious and asked him exactly where they lived. Barry described the house. George asked him to describe the ladies.

"One was big and fat, pretty face but too much weight. The odda one look good man, great shape but a really large behin'."

George got excited. "My Gad!" He said, "nuh Doris and Cherry."

A frown crossed his face. "Dem come back from Englan' a'ready?" He shook his head in disbelief.

"Dem married?" Barry asked, not wanting to seem to be inquiring about Doris in particular.

George laughed. "Tom will kill yuh fi him wife. An' mi nah talk 'bout de fat one."

Barry was very disappointed. "Who is Tom?"

"Tom is the bigges', baddes' man dem have down a di banana plant. Him can lif' yuh up wid him likkle finga."

Barry laughed, making a joke of the matter but he was very disappointed and still looked forward to meeting the lady again.

That very evening, two ladies dressed in flowing white dresses boarded a British Airways plane bound for London, England. No one saw them board the plane, nor did anyone see them sit in two empty back seats. The only tell tale of their presence was the putrid smell of rotten flesh and the faint smell of Jasmine, passing through the cabin every now and then, disappearing as soon as it was noticed, and the intermittent giggles which were audible but could not be identified.

Mable Gauntly was worried when her daughters did not arrive on the plane that Sunday afternoon. She thought maybe they had missed the plane and would write to let her know when they would be coming. As the days passed, she became more worried, no letter, no phone call, no word at all. At the end of the week, she wrote, asking them to call her; there was no reply. On the third Sunday, since their planned arrival, Mable decided to ask the local police in London. She wanted them to call Jamaica and inquire about the whereabouts of her daughters. She was certain something awful had happened. She planned to go to the police station first thing Monday morning.

That night her head hardly hit the bed when she fell asleep and had a dream. In the dream, she saw her daughters dressed in black walking down the road. She looked around and realized they were in Jamaica. She was about to ask them why they had not come to London when the doorbell rang. Mable felt dizzy. She wasn't sure if she was still dreaming or actually answering her doorbell.

Ms. Gauntly opened the door to the sound of laughter and there before her were her two daughters dressed in beautiful white gowns, giggling at each other. She rushed to hug them just as her youngest daughter's head slid from its body and hit the ground. Mavis screamed but no sound came from her frozen lips and she fainted. It was her neighbour who found her lying, unconscious, in the wide-open doorway. He rushed to her side, lifted her, took her inside, and placed her gently on the bed.

She awoke a few minutes later with a splitting headache. By then Cedric, her neighbour, had coffee brewing, she looked around smelling the coffee and, wondering what had happened, walked cautiously towards the kitchen.

"What happened?" asked Cedric.

"Don't know. How did you get in? What's happening?"

"I found you in the doorway unconscious."

Then she remembered the dream.

"I was having a terrible dream. I must have walked in my sleep, opened the door and fainted."

"Looks like it to me," he said, a little mystified. He handed her a cup of coffee and retained a cup for himself.

"Tell me about the dream."

"It was about my daughters in Jamaica, but I can't remember the details."

"But you said it was a bad dream. What made it bad?"

"I don't know."

He did not prod her any further. They drank the coffee and she began to feel better - much better. He looked at her closely; she looked fine.

"You'll be ok now -I hope?"

"Yes! Yes, I'll be fine."

He left and closed the door behind him. No sooner had he walked out, her head began to spin and she felt dizzy. She shook her head, fighting the fatigue, but the feelings persisted. Slowly, she walked towards her room and fell full length across the bed; she was asleep in no time. At first, the sleep was deep and undisturbed. Then the dream began to take shape: both daughters were fighting with Tom Francis. They wanted vegetables for dinner but he said no. Both girls grabbed him and pulled him to the vegetable garden and forced him to uproot the carrots and cabbages. The air was full of laughter as each plant came up with blood on its roots, only Tom was not laughing. Root after root of vegetable had blood on them until nine roots were counted. Then, the tenth root came up with nothing, not a sign of blood. The girls playfully pushed Francis to the ground and disappeared into the house.

Ms. Gauntly awoke frightened, she immediately knew what had happened - her daughters were dead; killed by Tom Francis and buried in the vegetable garden behind the house. The next day she walked to the police station and reported the double murder. No one believed her but she insisted they call Jamaica. She had proof that she had sent her two daughters plane tickets over a month ago. They were never used.

The call came from London to the Highgate police. Inspector Riley took the call and placed himself in charge of the case. Initial investigations revealed that both ladies had left for England well over a month ago. He informed the London police who, for the first time, agreed that something was wrong. They called Ms. Gauntly in for questioning and for the first time she told the police about her dream and suggested where to look for the bodies. Not taking any chances the London police called Highgate and instructed the police to dig up the vegetable garden. The police dug up the eight pieces of Cherry's body, each piece badly decomposed, and finally Doris' head and body.

That Sunday the sisters were nicely dressed in beautiful white gowns and given a proper burial. All Highgate turned out to say goodbye to these two unfortunate ladies. They were put to rest - at last.

Barry could not believe it; he had transported two Duppy sisters from Highgate to Kingston that Monday morning. He swore he would never give a lift to another stranger for the rest of his life. The sisters were never seen again but, every now and then, people reported hearing giggles coming from the house on the hill.

Tom Francis was tried in the Spanish Town courthouse and convicted of the double murder of the Gauntly sisters. He died, in the penitentiary, of a heart attack, six o'clock one morning, two weeks before he was due to be hung.

The story was so intense and serious that even my mother, who heard it before, sat starry eyed. Mrs. Kaneohe pulled the plaid scarf over her head in an attempt to hide the dread she felt and which was apparent in her eyes. This beautiful, timid Native American woman was shocked at the ruthlessness of the story, not having experienced anything close to such viciousness before. Sure, she had read stories much more vile than this one - like the fights between her people and the white man who invaded their lands. She knew of the scalping of people but to her, those incidents were far away and took place mostly during war times. This bloody story seemed much, much closer home to her, especially hearing it, firsthand, from someone who lived it and knew it actually happened.

Ms. Kaneohe was pale and so were her sons, except they were afraid while she was appalled. My father laughed out loud.

"Hey," he intoned, "that was over thirty years ago. Since then much, much worse has happened in Highgate."

"Like what?" asked Carmen a bit frightened.

"Dat's a story for another time, we've had enough for tonight. Mek wi meet again next storytelling time, same place, same time."

A bit shaken I got to my feet. No way was I going to my room alone - two terrifying stories in one night? No, it was more than I could take. Luckily, my sister's bed was just across from mine in the same room. Together, we walked to our room. I must have had ten nightmares through-out the night.

Next day, I reviewed the story, slowly running the terrible events through my mind. I figured I was a sadist, gluten for punishment, because I could hardly wait for the next Highgate Duppy story. I also realized all my friends were equally awaiting the first Saturday night in August, at the end of summer 1951. Only ma wasn't so anxious. She knew I was getting hooked, literally drugged by daddy's fantastic stories.

Chapter 3

*W*hen my daddy took his usual seat on the highest step of the stairs leading to our veranda he knew his occupation, as a storyteller, had grown to become an imperative feature in the lives of many friends in Belle Glade.

A large crowd had gathered anxious to listen to his tales of duppy, obeah, or murder. Only a little over a year had past and, in this meager period of time, he had become respected as the local griot, the teller of duppy tales and the keeper of Highgate's oral traditions.

Daddy's masterful storytelling skills extended itself to an unsophisticated way of promoting his future stories. He sought simple incidents, at any time of day or night, to promote upcoming stories. For example, he'd point to a mango tree and say, "See dat Mango tree? Dere was a big mango tree in Highgate where two duppy use to live. A will tell yuh 'bout di mango duppy dem nex' time."

Or, he might be walking along and, noticing a bird he'd say something like, "See dat bird, 'im could be a duppy bird yuh nuh. Dere was a duppy bird like dat in Highgate an' 'im use to give people hell. Nex' Saturday mi tell yuh 'bout di duppy bird."

This caused our friends to seek insight about the upcoming story and spread the word like wildfire; Mass Lester was going to tell a story about this or about that. Everyone would look forward to his story with great anticipation.

I really enjoyed storytelling and was doing pretty well narrating my own stories to school friends. None of them were about Highgate - those were left for my father's Saturday night sessions. I hoped one day to become as good a storyteller as he and couldn't understand why mama didn't want me to follow in his footsteps. Couldn't she see how I could work and tell stories just like daddy? Didn't she know it was my calling, just as it was daddy's and his fathers before him? I was too young to realize mama was looking into future America.

Storytelling was a dying art and mama understood it. Daddy was too set in his ways, to see and acknowledge this simple fact. In those early days, mama saw the Americans, white Americans in the southern states, struggling to hold on to even the tiniest vestige of slavery. She taught me early that the southern white man depended on plantation life to maintain his aristocratic lifestyle while northerners were experiencing the industrial revolution and needed more skilled laborers for their survival.

Mama realized the north was the harbinger of future America and wanted a northern lifestyle for her son. She confided in me her desire to send me to college in New York, a prospect I shuddered to even think about though I did not let her know this. Mama saw us as a part of a growing world, as a segment of a race of people out of Africa distributed throughout the world. Some were in Jamaica and the Caribbean while others were in America and the other parts of the world. On the other hand, daddy was living easily, doing his thing, the way he liked, without undue concern for civic or social issues. Like mama though, he saw himself, not only as Jamaican, but a part of the wide collection of African peoples spread throughout the Diaspora. Being a Jamaican, he felt connected to all people of African origin especially African Americans.

I liked Daddy's outlook and lifestyle and I especially remember the Saturday of April 18th, 1953 when I visited Fort Lauderdale. It was the first Saturday in April and we were looking forward to an exciting night of duppy stories but Daddy had to purchase various supplies in Fort Lauderdale, one of the bigger cities in South Florida. At thirteen, he felt I was old enough to go shopping so, for the first time, he took me with him. I was overwhelmed by the large resplendent city: its mighty buildings, huge undulating waterways, its luxurious yachts, small boats and barges, its splendidly dressed men and women, and the general hustle and bustle of downtown.

We took a taxi from uptown to the downtown section where Daddy needed to purchase the products. The flabby, untidy, white taxi cab driver engaged Daddy in conversation by first asking where we were from.

"Jamaica," daddy answered laconically.

"Boy - your son?"

"Yes sah."

"Nice boy. You must be proud of him, eh?"

The compliment opened my father's appetite for conversation. "Sure I'm proud of him. One day, he's going to be a great storyteller like me."

"You a storyteller?"

"Yes sir."

"Where do you live?"

"Belle Glade," I ventured

"So you are Jamaicans living in Belle Glade, eh?"

"Yes sir," daddy replied.

A broad smile lit up the driver's swarthy, bearded face. "Been to Jamaica once in the early forties while the war was going on. Got hurt in Europe and was sent home. Needed a little relaxation and went to Jamaica. Stayed in a place called Montego Bay. Know Montego Bay?"

"Yes," daddy said, remembering the time he worked there for three months.

"Beautiful place, very nice people."

"Yep," daddy said, "Jamaicans love foreigners and treat them well."

"Why do you leave such a beautiful country to come here to live?" The taxi driver asked.

Daddy was quiet for a while. This was not one of his favorite questions and he wondered how to answer it.

"Can make more money here," he said simply.

"I know. People are pretty poor over there - eh? Can hardly get a proper place to live or food to eat. Mostly ghetto - eh? Like in Kingston. I spent a few days in Kingston. The place was nice, but dirty and too much poverty."

I was beginning to feel a little uncomfortable and I noticed that daddy was also not that comfortable. After all, it's not as if Jamaica was a poverty stricken place with only poor people. To me, America was not a great deal better - just bigger with more opportunities for poor people. And opportunity meant work, not necessarily luxury but hard day-to-day work which was not readily available in Jamaica. Even at thirteen, I still remembered many beautiful places in Jamaica, nice big houses that looked better than many I saw in America - and many rich people too. They dressed just as nicely. But this taxi-man, who I was getting to dislike, made it seem like Jamaica was a place filled with only poor people who couldn't find work.

The driver noticed daddy's sombre mood and continued.

"But you Jamaicans are not like the American Blacks over here. You are good people. Better people. Not like these lazy good for nothings who don't want to work. They are always complaining about slavery. Everything to them is slavery. It's like the world owes them something."

Daddy was getting real angry and I noticed it. He was thinking of the hard working African American men and women of Belle Glade. Those who were underpaid by their white employers, who many times were forced to stay away from the farms they worked on. I too was thinking along those lines. I remembered what happened in Belle Glade just before we arrived earlier in the forties: two prominent Belle Glade African American men, funeral home owner W.C. Taylor and businessman J.T. Houston, were responsible for preventing one of the biggest exigencies in the sugar cane industry. Along with two prominent whites, the Rev. J.O. Jameson and George Royal, a businessman, these goodly men and others met and suggested to the farmers in the area that they pick men from among the workers to act as crew leaders. These leaders were responsible for wage negotiation and dealing with other issues with farm owners. It was only because of this plan that the underpaid hard working black men and women returned to the fields. If this had not happened, the crops wouldn't have got picked that year.

It was because of these men, yes black African American men included, that other racial issues were addressed making it possible for me, my father and other blacks, to live peaceably in Belle Glade without the Ku Klux Klan and other racists burning crosses and lynching us.

I remember how proud my mother was as she spoke of our African American brothers who started the state's second Inter-Racial Council. They held their first meeting on April 4th - the very year we arrived 1948. Mama read everything about the council she could get her hands on and she proudly told us what was going on. She said the council's bylaws stated that the membership would consist of fifteen blacks and fifteen whites with each member having an equal vote.

It was the council that convinced the Palm Beach County School Board to build a new elementary school for Belle Glade's black community. The members established a day-care centre for black children. It was through this council that a park, a playground and a swimming pool were built for the black Belle Glade neighbourhood. Even black police officers were appointed through their efforts. Yes, it was black people too who fought for every liberty and any progress that we achieved and this white Taxi man, who did not know or simply forgot, dared to call our African American brothers 'lazy good for nothings who don't want to work who always complained about slavery'. I listened as he continued:

"Them American blacks don't like you foreigners either. They say you are just taking away their jobs. That's because you know how to work hard and they don't. Give them a job and they don't want it or they want a million dollars for a few hours work. Look at me for example. I drive my taxi for a living but the worthless black people are always begging. I wouldn't give them a cent. Yes sir, you people are different. I like you man. I like you."

It was good for him that we reached our destination because I didn't know what daddy would have said to him. The fat taxi-man pulled his car close to the curbside. We alighted and my father, feeling in his pocket for the taxi fare, stared meanly at him and said, "I don't want you to like me man. If you don't like my brothers you can't like me."

The fat white man was shocked. He barely wanted to stretch his hand for his money but daddy wasn't finished with him yet. Holding the dollar bills in his outstretched hand just out of the Taxi man's reach and continued. "I am just as lazy and good for nothing as they are. Got it?" He stretched his hand closer and the man plucked the money from his hand and pulled the cab away from the curb, wheels screaming on his way. Daddy laughed and looked at me. He knew as young as I was, I understood. Maybe not everything but enough.

"We have to mek haste and shop so we can get back in time fi story time son. Yuh waan fi late?"

"No Daddy," I responded brightly, remembering this was first Saturday of the month. We walked briskly to the shopping area and bought our supplies. Three hours later, we were back at the shop.

The little shop had been expanded to include a clothes section and a little bar over which my father paid the greatest attention. Mother helped to unpack most of the supplies for the clothing section while daddy and I unpacked the rest. I was very excited as evening pushed closer. We all knew what tonight's story was about. Last Wednesday, a few of daddy's friends and a passing stranger were having a drink when two young people, holding hands, came into the shop. Daddy looked at them and inquired.

"Heny a yuh know dem young people deh?"

"Yep," said one of his friends. "Is Mr. Peterson daughter and di bwoy come from somewhere upstate - Fort Myers a t'ink."

"A hope dem young lovers know 'ow fi protect dem self if one a dem should die," my father said. "In Jamaica, people know 'ow fi protect dem self against dem love ones after dem dead. Rememba, young people can dead to, yuh nuh have to be ol'. Everyone have fi learn fi protect dem self from duppy. Henyway come Saturday evening, me tell unno a story 'bout two lovers."

Word spread rapidly. Daddy was going to tell a duppy story about two lovers. So, as we sat there, we knew it would be Lester, the storyteller, who would occupy the top step. And Lester told one of the most terrifying yet beautiful stories about two lovers. As usual Daddy claimed it was a true story. He said it took place in the little district of Cromwell Land, a suburb of Highgate in the parish of St. Mary, Jamaica. He called the story "The Lovers".

Daddy calmly began in his most polished English, and we listened attentively as he spoke.

The Lovers

Toby walked into the study just as Ruth Stern sat gingerly on the expensive Victorian sofa usually reserved for special guests. A slight tell-tale sign of pain crept across her face. Not being one to bring attention to her discomfort, she smiled and spoke directly to him.

"Where is Mr. Stern, Toby?"

"In the kitchen Ma'am."

His shadow, appearing on the walls at the far side of the room, was accompanied by his loud and thunderous voice that seemed to fill the room.

"So my dear, you are up! How is the foot today?"

"Not so good Reuben."

She pulled her left foot towards her, moving her knee in an upward arc. Reuben saw the pain in her eyes and noticed the sofa she was sitting in. He immediately knew the pain had forced her to sit in the first convenient place. The big man felt uncomfortable, he did not know how to help and felt clumsy touching any part of her body in an effort to relieve pain.

Toby saw it too, the pain, the discomfort, the concern, the fright. Yep! All those emotions registered, so he hobbled to her side. His own right foot did not allow him to walk normally having lost two toes in the war. He swore he would never practice medicine again; but what the hell, he would only use Jamaica's bush medicine. That's not like it was in the war; being a medic or anything like that; so he spoke unhurriedly.

"Do you mind sir, if I wash and massage your wife's foot?"

Reuben looked at him in surprise and chuckled.

"What does a chauffer know about massaging a sick foot, my good man?"

"Mr. Stern," he replied, "I was not always a chauffer sir. During the war, I was a medicine man. Even more so sir, I actually studied medicine though I did not get any degree."

The big Jewish man looked at the slender ill-fed black man with new interest.

"Ok Toby," he said walking through the door, "take good care of her for me."

Toby bent and felt her feet; he knew immediately. It was arthritis. "Don't move," he ordered, I will be right back."

He limped as fast as he could to the garden. There, he gathered some bushes: Sarsaparilla, excellent for arthritis, Dandelion which Jamaicans called 'Piss-a-bed', great for any skin disorder, and Leaf of life, used for swelling. Toby rubbed them all together and placed the mixture in a basin with warm water. He rubbed and mixed in some Ramgoat roses - a complete mix to ensure a perfect cure. When he got to the room, she was dozing. He gently lifted and placed her left foot in the basin. She jerked to full consciousness as the warm mixture hit her foot. Then she lay back and allowed him to massage her foot, from her toes to her knee.

"You are an expert," she whispered, "I never knew you know anything about bush medicine or massaging."

Her eyes were closed; he stared intently at her face without pausing the massage. Toby knew she did not expect an answer and did not offer one. He stared admiringly at the black hair, only speckled with grey, flowing to her shoulders. One hundred and five pounds, he guessed, not a sign of fat anywhere. He wondered how this was possible. How on earth could a white Jewish woman look so good at seventy years of age? Her legs were beautiful, without scar or wrinkle, though her face revealed signs of her age. Only rich white people can live like this, he thought, rubbing her ankles vigorously. After three minutes, the pain subsided and she felt pacified; her world was perfect as she slept.

It was a cool Wednesday morning, April seventeenth, nineteen thirty-five, exactly one month and a fortnight since her first massage, and exactly one year since Toby took the job as their chauffer. The first day of massage had partially healed her foot and, after two massages per week, she was pain free and completely healed. Still, he was exceptionally competent and, because it felt so good, she simply had to have at least one massage per week. He was promoted from chauffer to nurse/chauffer, with the added duties of a regular nurse. He finished massaging her feet when suddenly the housemaid, Puncy, burst into the room.

"Miss Ruth come quick, Mass Reuben sick bad. Him in di room cyaan move Mam. Come now."

Without a word, they both followed the maid to Reuben's study where he lay motionless on the couch.

"Puncy, tell Johno to hitch up the horses to the carriage immediately," Toby commanded.

Ruth rushed to her husband's side and with tears in her eyes, hugged him, whispering in his ears.

"Speak to me Reuben. Please Reuben, be ok. Reuben! Reuben! Reuben!"

Toby looked at Reuben's closed eyes. He noticed the yellowish froth forming at the corners of his mouth. He quickly placed the back of his hand to Reuben's neck. The big man's skin felt hot to the touch.

"He has a fever," Toby said to Ruth.

Walking as fast as his bad legs would allow him, Toby scrambled to the kitchen. He looked in the cupboard and found what he wanted - Bamboo leaf. He vigorously mixed it with some guinea grass and white rum. This should cure the fever, he thought. He went to Reuben's side and, using a teaspoon forced the liquid down his throat.

"Bay Rum," he shouted.

Puncy was back in a jiffy, handing him the Bay Rum bottle. He rubbed the big man's face and chest with the medicine. He knew Reuben had malaria but something else was wrong; somebody must be working guzzu on the boss. Yes! Obeah is a part of it, or else why the sudden unconsciousness and why the yellow froth? He had seen it before and each time the person had died in a short time. The thought had hardly crossed his mind when Reuben opened his eyes and moved his head away from the sting of the Bay Rum. He smiled weakly.

"We must take him to the doctor in Highgate," Ruth said.

Toby directed the two-horse team pulling the big black buggy with Reuben and Ruth in the carriage to the office of Dr. Timothy James. The small and kindly white man from Dublin, England, diagnosed Reuben's illness as malaria but said there were complications of which he was unsure. He gave Reuben some medicine and they returned to the big house in Cromwell Land.

For two weeks, Reuben was ill. The fever had broken and the malaria was gone, thanks to Toby's medicine and loving care, but still, Reuben got weaker and weaker. Dr. James could not say why and Toby's many visits to three local obeah men were unfruitful. None of them could do anything about it saying it came directly from a powerful source overseas called DuClarence, a dreaded servant of the Sasabonsam.

The constant trips from Cromwell Land to the doctor's office in

Highgate also did not help the rapidly deteriorating Reuben Stern. Although the cushiony leather seat of the buggy was comfortable, the clikerty, clikerty, clap, clikerty, clikerty, clap of Hadrian and Marcus (the horses), and the unavoidable sideway movement of the carriage made him worse when the trip was over. Sometimes, the horses trotted a little faster than he liked but Toby kept Hadrian and Marcus at their usual pace and Reuben said nothing. At the end of the second week, Reuben died.

Ruth took over the affairs of the estate with little interest. Nevertheless, she tried to encourage the workers.

"Reuben is gone," she said, "but we must carry on."

She never believed in the obeah theory and said so openly. And she would not encourage any talk about it. Toby, on the other hand, knew full well what had happened.

Many of Reuben's workers and friends within the district of Cromwell Land wanted to hold a Nine Night, but Ruth would not allow such activity in the house. Her daughter and a few relatives convinced her to allow a less extensive event than normal. She agreed to a Nine Night confined to the outdoor shed. Many locals complained bitterly. Throughout the parish of St. Mary, it was the custom to hold a Nine Night when anyone died and the main activity must take place in the dead person's room. In this case, it should be Reuben's room. They had planned to build a triple-tiered altar in his room with a glass of water on each level. Beside the water, they would place three black and three white candles, with a vase of flowers and Reuben's photograph on the top level. Mass Claude would preside and just before midnight all relatives and friends would light the candles and say a few kind words about Mass Reuben.

Ruth Stern wanted to have no part of this, especially after Toby explained that at midnight, Reuben's spirit would appear through Mass Claude or someone in the room. As he explained, it is through this medium Mass Reuben would tell them what happened to him and why he died. Toby said if Mass Stern's spirit did not come forward, they would have to burn coal and place some ashes in a pan and throw frankincense and myrrh on the coals to compel him to appear. Once he appeared and gave his story, everyone would march out of the house singing "Rock of Ages".

Ruth was secretly afraid and did not want to talk about Reuben's spirit at all. More than anything else, she did not want his spirit to be disturbed. But Toby assured her that they would not be disturbing Mass Stern's spirit, because nine days after burial the soul departed from the earth and it was not good if friends and relatives did not bid the departing soul farewell. This piece of advice frightened her and she wanted to know more about the planned event.

Toby was concerned about Ruth's health and knew she was afraid. He spoke to her gently.

"Don't worry about it. If you are a little afraid, then stay with Connie and your family in the living room while we set the spirit free."

"What do you mean, set the spirit free?" she whispered. Toby being the only person she could speak to freely and dare to show any weakness.

Toby sighed, "It is our custom, Miss Ruth."

"Toby," she said shivering a little, "explain what happen during the rest of the Nine Night, please."

"Well," he began, "after we gather, the official prayer and speeches will start. Mass Claude will lead the singing of the hymn and sanky. Some of the people will start to sing for food, then we will serve coffee and chocolate tea. Those who want rum or beer can have it. People love fried fish and hard-dough bread and Puncy will cook the white rice. But she can't put any salt in it."

"Why no salt?"

"Because spirits don't eat salt or anything wid salt. Anyway, after we sprinkle some of the white rum on the ground for Mass Reuben, we decide on which games we want to play while others sing. Remember, Mass Claude will be in charge of the singing. We will continue all night until next morning. At daybreak, some of the people will take the glasses from the altar and throw the water in the road. Others will turn over the mattress; sweep the house and burn or give away all of the Mass Reuben clothes you don't want. Then Mass Reuben's spirit will be set free - forever."

Ruth shivered, feeling a chill despite the simmering heat. She hugged herself, smiled and thanked Toby.

"Toby I ask only that you control the people. Tell them to do anything they want down by the shed but I can't stand any Nine Night in the house. I will provide the drinks and food, anything they want but no visits to the house. Ok?"

"Yes, Miss Ruth I understand."

On the ninth day, they extended the shed and prepared an altar. They took the mattress from the bed and placed the bed on the other side of the room to protect Miss Ruth. The Nine Night began in earnest at about eleven thirty that evening. At seventy, Ruth Stern couldn't shake the fear of death she had developed on migrating to Cromwell Land, Highgate, St. Mary some fifty years ago. Reuben had married her and taken her to this lovely town with its beautiful people. But nowhere else had she ever seen people use the machete as a fighting tool, beheading others, or simply to cut off a hand or a foot. And, nowhere else were there more rumors about obeah. Yet, the people were friendly, giving no one any cause to fear them - until of course they died. Today, she was grateful to her daughter, a few family members and other close friends for keeping her company. They had been with her since Reuben passed away and planned to stay for a few weeks.

No one wanted to sleep in the bedroom that she and Reuben shared. There were six other rooms where her guests slept. She herself preferred to sleep on the settee. That night, they all went to bed late, visiting the shed and mingling with the people for just about an hour after the Nine Night had began. It was shortly after four in the morning before Ruth finally fell asleep. She was tired and the constant singing lulled her to a fragile slumber. Five minutes into the sleep, she had the distinct feeling that someone had sat on the settee at her feet. She slowly opened her eyes but there was no one. She tried as hard as she could, but the powerful feeling of not being alone pervaded her very being. Then she smelt it, just a whiff at first. Then it became stronger and more overpowering; it was the smell of his cologne -the very one they buried Reuben in. She saw nothing but felt the cold touch and screamed, running from the room as fast as she could.

Her daughter was the first by her side holding her, comforting her, yet trying to understand what had happened.

"He is here," she sobbed.

"Who is here?" they all asked.

"Reuben," She cried, "why won't he leave me alone?"

They all looked at each other and gently led her to her daughter's room where they all huddled together for the night. No one at the Nine Night, especially not Toby, knew what had happened. For weeks, each time she decided to sleep alone she knew someone else was with her, either by a cold touch, the overpowering smell, or both. Sometimes, even when she was with someone, the presence was there. Finally, she could take it no longer and called Toby.

"Reuben is with me every night." She told him.

"What! How do you know?"

She told him what had happened the night of the Nine Night and gave him details of the other incidents. He frowned and spoke cautiously.

"Did they tell you to wear red underwear turned on the wrong side for three nights after Mass Reuben passed?"

"My God no! What are you saying Reuben?"

"So you have not done that eh?"

"No, I don't even own a red drawers."

"Then buy one and for the next three days wear it on the wrong side. After that, he will go away forever."

So she went to the little store down the road and purchased two cheap red panties. When she got home she changed, pulling the panty on the wrong side. For three days, she wore the panties as she was told. From the first day henceforth, she never felt Reuben's presence again; he was indeed gone.

The next six months were challenging ones for Ruth. Luckily, she had Toby to help her. Then, one day, it hit her like a ton of bricks. At seventy years of age, she was in love with the sixty year-old half crippled black man -Toby.

At first she felt confused, then it became clear. From the first day he offered to massage her ailing feet she had fallen in love with him. She did not realize it then because Reuben was alive. He was her all - her life. After his death, things were too hectic and she had no time to even reflect on it. But there it was; this feeling of need, of wanting to be with him, to talk to him, just to be around him. You old fool, she thought, what are you thinking about? I'm too old a woman to be feeling or thinking this way. And what about him? Yes! What about Toby? He is a younger man though not very young, about ten years younger than me. Will he ever be interested? She made up her mind then and there: she would write a simple letter to him. She would tell him she loved him but would not hold him to returning her feelings. He was free to do as he wished.

Toby received the letter that bright Friday morning of June twenty eight, nineteen thirty-five. It was hand delivered by Sharon Tate, Ruth's best friend. She handed it to him the minute he drove the carriage into the yard. Her smile and quick departure caused him much curiosity. He opened the letter immediately. My God, he thought, it can't be. Oh, how he wished he had the slightest chance to be a husband to this beautiful lady whom he loved, so much, from the day he entered her house. Now she was confessing her love for him. Toby sat on the carriage for five full minutes mulling over the turn of events. Then he decided; yes I'll go to her and let her know how I feel.

He found her sitting on her favorite chair. He held the opened letter in his outstretched, trembling hands. "Do you mean what you wrote here?" he managed.

With tears in her eyes, she shook her head slowly, ever so slowly that he wondered if he was imagining it. He took a few unsteady steps towards her, but she was already in his arms.

For the next two hours, they spoke of what had happened in their lives and what could have been. He wanted to know her plans and told her of his desire to marry her, but she reminded him of his wife, that she was neither dead nor were they divorced. She smilingly pointed out that they simply couldn't get married.

"Of course we can," he responded enthusiastically. "I'll go to England, find her and get a divorce."

"No dear," she said, holding his hand and squeezing it to her breast, "how much time do you think we have together? I'm an old woman now. By the time you get to England and back, I'll be gone. We would have wasted all that time and I couldn't bear you being away."

"But I want us to be married," he replied, "in three or four months I'll be back and all will be well. You have many more years to live. Three months won't kill us."

"Do you realize, Toby, while Reuben was alive I was strong? I could do anything, go anywhere, and manage anyone. Then when he departed, you were there; again I was strong. I know I would survive, I would manage, but that's because you were there, I could lean on you. Yes Toby, in many ways you took the place of Reuben. Now if you should leave, even for a month, I simply couldn't manage. I know I couldn't make it. Do you understand? I couldn't make it without you. So let's make the best of our lives, for as long as it lasts."

Toby was quiet for a long time. Then he stepped one pace back from her.

"What will your daughter think? What will the rest of family think? And your friends, what will they say? You know what they will say about you, don't you? They will say: 'Yuh si that rich white woman, Ruth Reuben? Yes! That pretty old lady, she's going with her black chauffer. Her, her, her, her half crippled chauffer'," he stammered.

She smiled and stepped towards him and placed her head on his chest.

"They are happy for me Toby. I told them all, before I told you; I had to. Not that it matters how they think, but I wanted to know. Of course, I knew my daughter would be happy. Connie is no fool; she sensed how I felt long before I even realized it. At least, so she told me."

"I see," was all he said.

She moved her head from his chest and stared into his eyes. "Please promise me one thing Toby," she asked.

"And what is that dear Ruth?"

"Never lie to me, ever Toby. Say only what you mean. Please mean everything you say, or, do not say it at all."

"That's an easy promise to keep dear, especially as I am not proned to lying. I'm too old for that. Yes! I promise."

And so they spent most of the morning, talking and enjoying each other's company. Then Toby had to do his usual chores and left Ruth asleep in the couch.

The following day, Toby moved into one of the larger bedrooms. A bachelor for over ten years, after his wife left him for England, he did not have much to move. The small two bedroom house he owned in Harmony Hall, about two and a half miles away, was not worth much so he allowed his good friend Greasy to live there. After all, if he should die all he owned belonged to Greasy.

For the next three years, the two lovers spent every minute they could together. They were very happy taking trips to Kingston, visiting the zoo and behaving like teenagers. Ruth never knew so much happiness existed and Toby was unbelievably contented. He loved horse racing, though he always lost his money. Now with Ruth at his side, he won often and in large amounts. Of course, she always confiscated the winnings when it exceeded fifty pounds because, as she said, no chance should be taken with losing it back the same day. He loved to place the bundle of money in her hands and watch her. She would excitedly fold the bills and place them in her bag, just as a little girl would. But money was never Ruth's problem; she had more than she could spend in a lifetime.

One night, on one of their trips to the north coast, they walked along the beach holding hands. The light from the lodging house skimmed the water like colorful little snakes swiveling along. Here and there a frog croaked, otherwise no living thing was in sight, and there was no other sound other than the slight rolling of the waves. Ruth stopped abruptly, her long black and silver hair fluttered in a passing wind.

"Do you know why I love you?" she asked.

"No," came the simple reply.

"It's because I have never had anyone, not my mother, nor my father, nor even Reuben, show me the kindness and concern you did that day you first massaged my foot."

"It was nothing Ruthy," he replied, using the new name he had given her and which she liked so much.

"It was everything to me darling. Everything! Because of that I shall love you for the rest of my days. Not that I have many more days left, but whatever I have left are yours."

He pulled her to him and whispered:

"The rest of my days are also…"

She cut him off by placing her fingers across his lips.

"No dear, do not say it. Remember? Only the truth, say only what you mean and can live up to. Promise nothing and nothing is expected of you. Promise the world and you'll carry it on your shoulder."

He gently removed her fingers, "My dear Ruthy, you have made a cripple like me whole again and for that I will love you for the rest of my life. In life and in death, I will be with you forever."

"Do you mean that Toby?"

"Yes my dear, I do."

They spent a wonderful night together and returned to Cromwell Land the following evening. For nine years, Toby and Ruth enjoyed each other and became familiar figures in the town of Highgate. Then on Thursday, August third, nineteen forty-four, Toby was notified of his wife's death in England. For nineteen years, he made no contact with her or any of her relatives. Now, her deathbed wish was for him to attend her funeral. She had openly asked God to forgive her for deserting him and was now begging his forgiveness. He did not want to go but Ruth persuaded him.

He made arrangements to sail on the HH Kennedy, the following Friday, August eleventh. Early that morning Ruth fell ill. This gave him a great excuse for not going; certainly he could not dream of leaving her while she was sick. When he told her, she insisted he go anyway.

"I can't leave you like this," he cried, holding her hands while she lay in their bed.

"Its nothing Toby, just a fresh cold."

"No! Ruthy, I can't go."

"But you must dear. Help her; set her spirit free just as you did for my Reuben. Please go Toby, go and help her."

He looked in her eyes and knew she meant it; he had to go. He left her lying in bed. Toby Williams was the saddest man for the entire two weeks journey to England.

Immediately on arriving in London, he found the first telephone and called. Puncy answered the phone and told him Miss Ruth had gotten worse. They handed her the phone and she spoke with difficulty; he could hardly hear her whisper.

"Don't worry my darling, I will not die until you get back here. I will wait for you." He was maddened with fear.

"But how do you know?" he shouted at her for the first time, "you have no control over death."

He sensed her smile as she answered, "I'll be here. You take your time, I'll be right here."

He did not enjoy his stay, mostly because he had to play the hypocrite with his former wife's family, smiling and behaving as if he cared. But he didn't care. He wanted to get back to his Ruthy now...now!

He arrived on the island two weeks and three days after speaking to Ruth. Oh how beautiful Jamaica looked after the dusky England. He got a free call from the terminus. The phone rang many times but no one answered. He hung up and tried again. The phone rang eleven times before feeble hands released it from its cradle; then it fell. The same hand retrieved it and Ruthy voice said, "Hello darling, it's good to have you back." Then the phone went dead.

The taxi couldn't travel fast enough around the twisting and winding roads of the Junction. Up through Clonmell they went, until, at last, he arrived at the house in Cromwell Land. He paid the driver and hopped as fast as he could to Ruth's room. He burst in the room where they were all standing, surrounding her bed. Momentarily, her eyes opened and he knew she recognized him. Her lips parted in a little smile.

"What happened?" he inquired.

"She's been in a coma for five days now," said Connie.

"But, but she answered the phone this morning," he stammered.

They looked at him in disbelief. They remembered the phone ringing while everyone was having breakfast but it stopped just as Puncy was about to get it. Connie thought about it and realized it did ring a second time after breakfast, but she thought someone else had answered it -certainly not her mother. Now she was certain, indeed Ruth had answered it. He sat by her side while they left the room, one by one. Toby took her hands and felt the life in it. He knew she was aware of his presence, so he spoke to her softly. He told her he loved her, he told her how happy she had made him and he begged her not to go but she passed away silently while he cried.

Toby allowed the Nine Night to be held in the shed, and like Ruthy, he did not allow anyone in the house. Everything went just as it did when Reuben died, except Toby slept in their room. He was now seventy years old, the same age as Ruthy when Reuben passed. He slept alone and cried, over and over he cried. For days and weeks, he cried then one night he felt her by his side. The room was full with the scent of her perfume. He couldn't see her but he knew she was there. Night after night she made her presence felt. Soon, he was hearing sounds like someone walking. The presence became more and more aggressive, making frightening sounds and shaking the bed. He became afraid and stopped sleeping in the room. He knew of no way to stop a woman duppy from bothering her mate. No red drawers turned wrong side would help. The seventy-year old black man with the missing toes did not know what to do.

Toby Williams slept on the couch two nights straight. Then, on the third night he had a vision. In the vision, he was talking to the wind. He heard his voice distinctly say, "My dear Ruthy, you have made a cripple like me whole again and for that I will love you for the rest of my life. In life and in death I will be with you forever." The wind whispered back, "Do you mean that Toby?"

He looked around startled; he saw no one but he knew she was on the couch. He couldn't breathe; he tried to rise but couldn't move; he shouted but no sound came. Then he relaxed and said, "Yes my dear, I'll never lie to you, here I am with you forever."

They found him curled up on the couch, the most glorious smile on his face. Toby Williams had joined his Ruthy.

The crowd cheered when Daddy finished his story. Some openly wiped tears from their eyes while others stifled back strong, sorrowing emotions by stretching or shutting their eyes tightly, squeezing out any evidence of tears. But Daddy knew his story had hit many emotional cords. He looked at me and squinted, I squinted back, our secret way of communicating congratulations and job well done. I really wished I could be half as good as daddy. That night before I went to bed I spoke with him.

"Daddy how come I am hearing this story for the first time?"

Daddy smiled, "Mi grampa tell mi dat story long, long ago. Not even mi fadda ever heard it before. Grampa specially want me to pass it down to mi son. I will tell it to yuh again another time."

"But how did Granpappy know you would have a son daddy?"

My father slapped on one of his secretive smiles and said, "Never mind that Cecil. 'Im know jus' like I know yuh will have a son too."

"One day, yuh son will tell dese same story. Believe me Cecil, story-telling come down from generation to generation of men in wi family an' it will continue."

"Daddy, when can I tell a story?"

My father looked at me sharply, "Yuh want to tell a story Cecil? Yuh believe yuh can tell a story before all dem people?"

"Well, maybe," I said cowardly.

"Yuh not ready yet son. But someday yuh will tell people this same story and them will love it. Don't worry yuh will get yuh chance. One t'ing: don't tell dis story till mi gone. Mek it be the first story yuh tell after me gone."

"Gone where Daddy?"

"When mi dead son. Afta mi pass away."

I loathed when daddy spoke like this. I hated it when he spoke of dying. Sure I know we all must die, but daddy, my father? No, he wouldn't die anytime soon.

"Daddy why talk of death? You are still young and strong, why talk about death?" I asked stubbornly.

He laughed, shook his head and said: "You're correct mi son, but is mi duty to prepare yuh. Mi might not be able fi do it when mi want. Henyting can 'appen. Yuh agree?"

"Yes Daddy."

"Goodnight son."

"Goodnight Daddy," and he was gone.

I went to bed in deep thought, more excited, now than ever, about becoming a good storyteller.

Mama awoke early Sunday morning and made breakfast for us all. As

we sat eating her usual corn bread, grits, fried eggs, and bacon, she directed her attention to me.

"Son, I saw Miss McDonald yesterday."

I knew immediately what was coming. Miss McDonald was my High
School 10th grade teacher. She felt Tom Duke, a tall black boy from the
third class, was a bad influence on me. Even though Tom was a year older
than me, we enjoyed each other's company because he always wanted to
know about Jamaica and was one of my father's greatest fans. Tom was a
bit of a bully though, fighting and beating up other boys but, as long as we
were friends, I had no fear of any boy in our school. None of the boys
dared pick a fight with me and, so, I enjoyed the benefit of his company.
Behind his back, they called him Tom-Du and the Du was not shortening
for Duke, rather it was the shortening for dunce. The boy who started the
nickname had a scar across his jaw as a reminder.

Tom Duke, however, had a great advantage; he was a superb baseball
player. Teachers tolerated him because of his talent and the girls loved him
because of it. This simple fact helped to cement our friendship as I enjoyed
being seen in the company of Belle Glade's most beautiful sophomores.
So, on this bright Sunday morning, I knew what Mama was about to say.

"Well, Miss Mac said you are getting very popular in school. You don't
know a lick about baseball but you and the whole baseball team are friends,
especially Mr. Duke boy. You and him are the best of friends, I understand.
Is this true son?"

"Yes Mama, Tom is my friend but not the whole baseball team - just
Tom."

My mother stopped eating and watched as I speak. Daddy continued
to eat but I was certain he was listening to every word I said. My sister was
giggling as she remembered rumors about some girls and I; nothing serious, just that we were always seen together and one of the girls was sup-
posed to be my girlfriend.

"So Tom Duke is your friend eh?" Mama said sarcastically. I kept quiet
so Mama continued. "Tom Duke can play baseball well Cecil, he won't
have any trouble getting a scholarship and going on to college. How about
you? When you become a man, how are you gonna make life, get money
and take care of a wife and children?"

"I will find work Mama and I will become a storyteller like Daddy."

"What kind of work you will find? Cut cane over the cane belt -eh?"

"Isabel! Why yuh nuh leave di bwoy alone?" Daddy asked, his voice calm but brittle.

Mama continued without yielding to daddy's statement. "Cecil, the boy is bad company. Because of him you are falling back in your Math and English. Miss Mac said you failed English and only barely pass the Math. How can you amount to anything if you don't graduate from High School? Don't you want to go to college boy?"

No. I don't want to go to college. After I graduate from high school, I want a job in one of those offices downtown and I want to start telling stories, just like my father. That's what I want. But I didn't say that to Mama. Instead, I hung my head and said compliantly, "Yes Mam."

"Promise mi Cecil," she persisted,"promise you'll stop keeping company with that boy."

"Ok Ma," I said meekly. I did not know how I'd keep such a promise but my mother was no one to play with and I was not about to try.

Chapter 4

A Rainy Night

When the rain came tumbling down that bleak and dreary Saturday morning of June 4, 1955, I knew we were in for a unique experience once evening reached our four-bedroom dwelling. No way could we sit comfortable outside, around the veranda steps, as we've been doing so many Saturday nights before. That day, I watched mama and Carmen bustling around the kitchen preparing the tasty Jamaican fruitcake we all treasured.

I loved when mama stayed home, as she did today, paying Rena, the part-time worker, one and a half of a days salary to manage the business alongside my father. There was no end to the delicious snacks and fruits available while she was home.

As the day moved towards its predictable end, the tantalizing aroma of cake battled with the heavy scent of Jamaican white rum (used in cake-baking) for supreme occupancy of every room in the house. Clearly, it was a day of exceptional promises. But it did not turn out as I predicted and yet it was one of the most unique Saturdays since our arrival in this almost naked little town called Belle Glade.

At fifteen, daddy had still not allowed me to tell a duppy story in front of a major crowd. Whenever the weather prevented a large gathering, he'd allow me to tell the few people that gathered a story or two, otherwise he'd not allow it at all.

We gathered on our veranda early that Saturday evening. Darkness fell early, the sun having gone minutes before, leaving the moon to hide beneath the thick dark clouds. Only Carmen, Barbara, Mass Joe, my two Native American friends, and their mother visited us that night. I was happy for the small gathering, not only because of the inconvenience a large crowd would present during a rainy day like today, but also because I really wanted a chance to tell a story. I thought it would be an ideal time to tell it. My father only narrated stories he had experienced himself, or those passed down by his father, many of which came from his grandfather. This left the length and breadth of other tales I'd heard.

Mother invited us in the large living room where we sat, Native American style, on her heavily polished wooden floor. Before long, she and Carmen served the delicious cake and biscuits they made earlier. The lemonade was a little sour but tasted perfect with the sweet cake. We washed it down in delightful gulps.

The years had mellowed my mother. She no longer badgered me about my grades and allowed daddy to tell his stories without comments. It really started after a truck rammed unto a fruit stall downtown and sent her flying in the air hitting the side of a bench, splintering it with her huge buttocks. Luckily for her, she did not land on any other part of her body or she might not have been with us today. Mama spent two weeks in the hospital and told us her father came to her in a vision and told her to make the most of what she had. She interpreted his words to mean she should enjoy her family without bothering them relentlessly. Daddy was the greatest beneficiary of this new realisation, followed by me. Pamela was always her pet so nothing changed there.

My grades had also improved although I was now more determined to become a good storyteller than ever. This, as well as the fact that Tom Duke had gotten a baseball scholarship and moved on to another school, helped to pacify mother. She no longer had to worry about his influence over me. Last time we heard about Tom he was doing quite well but was still very backward, academically.

Anyway, that rainy evening, daddy came home over an hour late and declared he was not going to tell any duppy stories. Disappointment shot through the room like a plague and everyone murmured. Then mother saved the day. Out of the blue, her voice rang out:

> *J1Evenin' time,*
> *Work is over now is evenin' time*

Those of us who knew the song joined her.

> *We deh walk pon mountain,*
> *Deh walk pan mountain,*

Deh walk pan mountain side.
Mek we cook wi bickle pan di way,
Mek wih eat an' sing,
Dance an' play ring ding
Pan dih mountain side.

As we sang, those who didn't know the song caught on and joined in. We sang both verses and with each verse we shouted the chorus. It was precisely at the end of this song that father joined us, trotting merrily into the room with his usual soft smile. We cheered realizing my parents and their friend Carmen staged the entire charade.

Daddy sat on a chair beside mother and Carmen. He surveyed the sea of faces staring up at him, and, in his usual relaxed manner leaned far back.

"Well," he said mockingly, "since yuh enjoy di song so much how 'bout dis one?"

Every time mi 'memba Liza,
Waata come a mi y'eye,
When mi t'ink pan mi nice gal Liza,
Waata come a mi y'eye

Come back Liza, come back gal,
Waata come a mi y'eye,
Come back Liza, come back gal,
Waata come a mi y'eye.

We immediately joined in singing energetically, our lungs stretched to its limits. We sang, song after song, energy ripping through the room like electricity. Then my father's bony hands stretched out in a signal to stop. The room fell quiet; he smiled and began.

"Riggle me dis," he yelled, "riggle me dat..." Daddy paused for dramatic effect, "guess me dis riggle an' per'aps not."

"What does he mean by that?" asked Mojoe.

"That's what we say in Jamaican when we are about to ask a riddle," I replied.

"Riggle mean riddle," declared my ten-year-old sister, Pamela, her chubby face breaking out in an enchanting little smile.

A sneaky grin overshadowed my father's eyes as he tried hard to hide his satisfaction at Pamela's outburst. Then he continued.

"Guess dis riggle: 'Up chip cherry, down chip cherry, Nat a man can climb chip cherry.' What am I?"

I looked at my mother's smiling face, quietly inveigling her to give me a revealing sign but Daddy caught on.

"Isabel," he warned, don't tell dem.

"No Lester," she chuckled good-naturedly.

My mother's behavior towards daddy had changed tremendously over the last couple of years, especially since daddy had become a distinguished and extraordinary Jamaican duppy storyteller. Her bossy nature subsided, she seldom barked at him, and now bestowed a lot of love, kindness and gentleness on him. I believed, in addition to her dream, Mama was enjoying enormous comfort and security from managing our expanded shop, turning it into a lucrative business and providing sufficient money to satisfy our needs. This, and the respect she now got from her friends and the entire Belle Glade district, certainly made her content. Daddy felt she was getting old and that's why she was, according to him, 'behaving herself'. However, he was very pleased and showed it every chance he got.

Mother gave no hint at the solution of the riddle and our wild guesses were all fruitless. Soon, my father asked if we gave up but before we could answer, my mother interrupted.

"It's smoke," she said, "no one can climb smoke".

Daddy snarled and looked at her sternly, pretending vexation. He had become very skillful at creating the exact environment he needed; sometimes hostile, oftentimes terrifying, and other times relaxed. Now, he wanted us to believe he was angry and would punish my mother.

"Ok Isabel", he said, "I never ask yuh, but since yuh answer, yuh have to ask the nex' riggle."

Mama took a deep breath. This was a high time for her and Daddy knew it. She was quite good at asking riddles. She pulled her heavy weight to its full height, her fat face twisted in pretended concentration, her lips puckered in thought, then her eyes popped out triumphantly as an expansive smile spread across her ruby red lips.

"Ok," she said, "riggle me dis - riggle me dat - guess me dis riggle an per'aps not." She continued, "My father have twenty-five white horse in a row; if one trot all trot, if one gallop all gallop, if one stop all stop, and one cannot go on without the other."

I knew the answer but, for the sake of my sister and our visitors, pretended I had no idea.

"I know! I know!" exclaimed Carmen excitedly.

"Ok, tell wi," Mama challenged

"Rice grain."

"No."

Then my sister gleefully shot out: "Teeth, Mama Teeth."

"That's correct Pam," Mama said, using my sister's pet name, clearly happy with her wit.

Mother again went into her thinking mode but I suddenly remembered the story I wanted to tell. Daddy had made no attempt to allow me to tell any stories even though he knew that back home, in Highgate, I had my own duppy experiences and often traded many duppy stories with my friends.

Long ago, mother told me he promised to give me a chance to tell one of my stories. I thought this was the perfect time so I took the chance and held up my hand, like a child in school.

"I have a story, can I tell it daddy?"

"Is not story night, Cecil," he exclaimed.

"It's a short one daddy," I said excitedly.

"Alright, alright. Gwaan bwoy, tell yuh story."

I took a deep breath and gazed at everyone, making a funny face in an attempt to develop a scary atmosphere. The story I was about to tell was one I heard many times in Jamaica. I was confident it would be new to my Native American friends but was not sure my family heard it before. Was it a true story? I did not know but I intended to pass it on as gospel truth. After making certain I had created a scary atmosphere, I began.

"One day a man from Highgate died. His uncle, who lived in Hampstead a little town about five miles from Highgate, agreed to make the coffin. The family asked Mr. Manley, a close friend with a truck, to pick up the coffin for them.

"It was a gloomy day and rain clouds were thick in the sky, hiding the sun from every corner of the earth, when Mr. Manley drove off taking Mickey with him to help lift the coffin. On their way back with the coffin, the rain began in torrents getting heavier with each passing minute. Mickey sat in the truck front beside Mr. Manley, while the coffin rested in the open truck back covered with a piece of tarpaulin. As they drove along in the rain, they saw a man by the wayside thumbing a ride. Mr. Manley pulled the truck to a halt beside the hitchhiker.

"Jump in di back," he told the man,"no room in di front."

"As they rode along, the stranger decided to lie in the coffin to shield himself from the rain. He jumped in, closed the lid, and lay still.

"Well, on their way they saw another hitchhiker, getting wet, with arms extended thumbing a ride. Again, Mr. Manley instructed the good man to hop in. Effortlessly, he swung himself over the rail and landed in the truck back. He saw the coffin and, feeling a little uneasy, sat in the far corner away from it. As they traveled the rain subsided. The man in the coffin, no longer hearing the pitter-patter of heavy raindrops, pushed open the cover and stood up.

"Rain done fall yet?" he inquired, smiling at the newcomer.

I paused allowing the group to visualize the scene. Mama started to laugh in anticipation and everyone was looking at me attentively, the making of laughter clearly in their eyes spreading to their lips. Unhurriedly, I continued.

"The last hitchhiker now terrified, believing it was the dead getting out of the coffin, jumped out of the moving truck, and up the road he ran, like a mongoose on fire.

"Mr. Manley and Mickey claimed they saw the man running past the truck even though they were going about ninety miles per hour. They could not believe it. Mr. Manley turned to Mickey and asked:

"Nuh di man weh we jus' gi a drive, a pass we?"

As I finished the story, laughter filled the house. My mother held her stomach as she shook with laughter. Daddy wiped the tears from his eyes, my sister was in stitches and the two Native Americans were rolling on the floor, hysterical with laughter. Even I could hardly finish the story with a straight face.

When he caught his breath daddy hugged me and whispered, "Yuh got dem bwoy, yuh got dem. Dat was a funny story me bwoy; very funny an' mi like it."

After a few more riddles, daddy stood and stretched.

"Is bedtime now," he said.

Laughter was still in the air when we went to bed. I was very happy. "You are a good storyteller," daddy said, "One day, you will take over as the village storyteller."

That night, mama had a sober talk with daddy. "Lester," she said, "Our son is fifteen now, in two years he will be ready for college. We have to help the boy turn out to something. Maybe he won't become a doctor or a lawyer but there are many other professions he can learn. He is good at Math and maybe he can learn accounting or something like that. You agree with me?"

"Di bwoy can get a work at anyone a di company dem downtown when 'im leave school Isabel. Weh yuh a trouble yuhself so for?" 'Im a go be a great story tella! Yuh nuh see it Isabel? Yuh nuh see it?"

Mama shook her head sadly, then pleaded desperately, "But Lester, if he graduate and go to college he will have a better chance of gettin' a good job in any company downtown. He can still tell his stories, but he will be able to earn more money than if he don't graduate."

"A true but nuh worry yuh head so much man. Education is not all."

"How is it yuh t'ink he is such a good storyteller and yuh never allow him to be the storyteller one Saturday night?"

"Yuh mean, mek 'im stan' up before everybady an' tell a story? Mek 'im control a Saturday night?" he chuckled amusedly.

"Yes," she said tersely.

"Yuh t'ink 'im can do it?"

"Yes, he can."

"Eh, eh."

"Yes, last week I heard him telling Mojoe a story and he was good at it."

"But dat different, 'im ongle a talk to one s'maddy -not a whole crowd."

"Does it matter, eh? Don't yuh say the boy tek after you? He can do it. As you say, one day he will be better than you."

Daddy smiled then, and shook his head in agreement.

"I hope so Isabel, I sure 'ope so."

"But you have to give him a fair chance Lester. Times are changing. The younger folks will soon stop visiting people's house to listen to stories, especially duppy stories."

"What yuh saying Isabel? Dat people will soon stop listen to story, an' storytelling will soon done?"

"Maybe not altogether. But yuh nuh si TV and movie tekking over? Don't you see the young ones are spending more and more Saturday nights at the movies?"

"Dat's true. But dem still a listen to story. An' mi a depend pon people like wi son, fi mek sure dat dem learn di art good, keep it interesting, and mek we people enjoy we history through story. One t'ing me know, fi be a storyteller yuh eeda born wid it, or yuh don't. An' when yuh born wid it, nutten can stop yuh. It inna yuh bones, yuh blood and yuh can automatically do it good. Like our son Isabel; 'im born wid it."

"Then Lester, you will have to give him a chance to practice. And you will have to give him a chance to learn in school so he can keep it going."

"Eh, eh. Yes Isabel, I will soon give 'im a chance."

She shook her head in familiar amazement. "Lester I know I talk about this a lot but - don't you think if you use more English around the house it will help Cecil and Pam learn English better? Everyday you get up yuh use the same ol' bad language, like you proud of it."

"Yuh wouldn' know, but me proud a it. An' don't mi keep me promise to yuh? Don't mi use only English when mi a tell mi story dem?"

"That's true Lester. You really keep your promise. But you know is the children I t'inking of. You know they need help with English in school and the best way to help them is to see to it that they always talk and listen to good English."

"No Isabel, yuh a t'ink 'bout yuhself and yuh hoity toity frien' dem. An' yuh know me nuh care."

"All right, all right Lester. Let's leave it alone."

"Tenk yuh."

"So Lester, you will give the boy a chance soon eh?

"Eh, heh. Me will give 'im a chance."

Daddy knew, as a storyteller, I had to be groomed exactly as his grandfather had groomed him. He simply didn't have the knack and proficiency to do it. He wondered if he should just sit with me and teach me as his grandfather had taught him. The difference was, his grandfather knew how, and enjoyed speaking to his son and grandson but daddy didn't have the verve, the thirst or desire. All his proficiency and enthusiasm was saved for sitting before a crowd and wooing them with his own story. He sat there long after mama had left, his thoughts on Jamaica, Africa, storytelling, duppies and me. He ruminated things his grandfather had told him mulling over some of his most solemn speeches. He remembered the last time the old man had spoken seriously to him, not long before he passed away.

"Son," the old man had said to him, "each generation must pass along to di younger generation di human experience dem live in story form. Long, long ago in Africa," he had paused to spit, a yellow liquid spewing from his mouth spattering the ground, "an' maybe it still is going on, people gather to learn about t'ings dat happen before dem born. Yuh know why son?" he continued before daddy could answer, "it help dem prevent some of di mistakes the older head dem mek and it teach dem to deal wid problems di same way the older folks did.

"Dis been going on long before Jesus Christ and the Bible an' even before the picture writings dem call hieroglyphics." The old man had to rest at intervals and daddy had seen the desire, the urgency he had to get his story out, as if his very life depended on it.

"Yuh never ask me why I choose to tell mostly duppy stories, eh bwoy? Well to me is like medicine yuh nuh, an' is like di Bible. Is like medicine because some people don't believe dat duppy deh. But evil spirit and good spirit exist. An' when dem hear some of my stories they learn how to deal wid duppy an' can protect demself. Dem believe because many a di story dem a true, a nuh fable. Is like di Bible because it teach yuh how fi love and serve God. An' when yuh love and serve God, no duppy or evil intent in a wicked people mind can trouuble yuh. Yuh protected at all times. Remember weh mi seh son, dem cyaan hurt yuh because God is wid yuh."

Daddy mulled these words and promised to speak to me one day, just as his father had, but he never did.

Chapter 5

Danzo Guzmore

My mother was waiting for me, as she had waited so many times since we agreed I would take private lessons at the Lindsay's. The look on her face was the same familiar and predictable one she wore each and every time. I stepped into the house and waited.

"Sit down, Cecil," she said,"I have something to say to you." I sat down warily, watching her as she leaned against the couch, stretching her hand to hug its upper section while sitting on its arm. Her face was composed, her voice measured. I watched her and felt that this certainly wasn't one of her predictable moments after all. I sat still, anxiously, waiting.

"Remember last September we heard there was a terrible train crash in Jamaica?"

"Yes Ma," I said.

"This morning," she added, "Well…someone told us that your father's good friend died in that crash. You may not remember Danzo Guzmore but he was a very nice man and a good friend of ours."

I quietly waited for her to continue. I was certain this was not just to inform me about Danzo's death. There must be more to come.

"Your father will be going to Jamaica to visit Danzo's family and your uncle Roger."

"But the crash was from last September. Don't tell me he wasn't buried all this time mama." I said sarcastically.

She laughed, "No, no. He was buried but it's been a long time since your father saw his own brother and he want to see Danzo's sister and wife too."

"Why didn't he go from September mama, when he could have attended the funeral?

"Because we had no idea Danzo was in the train. It was long after the incident that we got the letter from your uncle. He said he mailed it as soon as he found out which was a couple of days after the crash but we got it weeks after they buried him."

Not moving, mama continued, "Would you like to go to Jamaica with your father Cecil?"

Was I hearing correctly? "What did you say mama?" I stammered. It was exactly the effect she wanted to have and she was pleased to see the utter surprise on my face.

"Your father agreed that you could go with him if you wanted. Do you?"

I was delighted and jumped from my seat to hug her. Ever since I came to America, I longed to go back to Jamaica. It had been eight long years and now I would have the chance to see my old friends and smell the banana trees as I did as a child. I hugged mama and then it hit me suddenly, like a punch square in my stomach.

"When is he going mama?" I blurted out nervously.

"Between now and the first week in December."

The excitement evaporated, leaving me limp. We were in the second to last week of November; two weeks time put us in the first week of December. "Oh Lord," I cried, "mama don't you remember the camp I am going to? The one in New York?" Her smile told me she remembered.

"We can cancel it. It's up to you."

I shook my head sadly, "I couldn't do that mama. I planned for it too long. Can't daddy put Jamaica off until I return from camp?"

She moved impatiently away from the couch, "That would be next year Cecil. I'm afraid he planned to go before Christmas. Next year, we have other things planned and, as you know, during Christmas time your father doesn't tell stories. It's his vacation time so he isn't going to change it."

"No Mama, I can't go," I said disgustedly, moving towards her and burying my head in her bosom.

"I know son," she crooned consolingly. But she didn't know. And I didn't want her to know that Dawn Cretin, my new girl friend, would be waiting for me in cold, cold upstate, New York where I was looking forward to seeing snow for the first time.

Kendal

y father spent a month in Jamaica during the fall of '57. When he returned he told me the most amazing story of his visit. But it was the story of the Kendal Train Crash and his friend Danzo. It kept me awake for many nights to come. This is the story my father relayed.

He arrived at the Palisadoes Airport, Kingston, in the scorching afternoon heat that raged despite the gentle sea breeze skipping across the nearby sands. Luckily, there were a few taxicabs on the stand, so he paid the man driving the sun burnt blue Buick to take him to Highgate. The car chirped along at an average of twenty-five miles per hour but daddy declared any motion in the broiling sun meant relief. He opened the passenger side window fully to allow the motion breeze to swirl through the car.

They ambled along merrily through the Kingston Sunday traffic, then the Buick picked up speed as it zipped down the steep and winding Stony Hill Road. Soon, they were throttling around the junction moving at a brisk pace. But it was not the motion of the Buick that daddy paid attention to, rather it was the unchanged, unspoiled, rich green grass and trees dressing the mountainside and timeless river called the Wag Waters. Many a time, his breath caught in his throat and he gasped at the magnificent sight before them. The rolling hills on the far side of the river with its light green grass blanket, its deep yellow, brown and green trees and the luscious, mouth watering mangoes, apples and plums hanging from laden trees.

Time and again, he asked Harry, the cab driver whom he became quite familiar with, to stop for him to purchase fruits, or to simply gloat and marvel at the stunning sights surrounding them. Daddy asked Harry if he drank alcoholic beverages. It seemed as if Harry was just waiting for such a question because he took it as invitation and blurted out, "We can stop round di likkle bar pan di way."

On Sundays, rum bars were not opened to the public but that did not stop locals from purchasing liquor and beers from the bars. They merrily entered from the back entrance regularly used by the proprietor and his staff and it was business as usual. When Harry led daddy into the little bar on the hillside, my father was back home indeed. At midday, the bar was steaming with life though the place seemed desolate from outside. They dove under the counter and pulled stools on the customer side where they sat amongst three other patrons. Daddy looked at the shapely barmaid with the inviting smile and ordered drinks for everyone.

"What about me?" she joked.

"Serve yuhself firs' sweetheart," he invited, generosity oozing from every pore, catalyzed by the atmosphere he loved and knew so well. But daddy was dealing with an expert. One look at his attire and the ringing of his semi-foreign accent told her all she needed to know; here was a loaded Jamaican from America. She snuggled up to him and before the day was done had literally taken over six dollars from him in drink, gifts and tips - an unusual practice in those parts. But daddy did not mind; he was home among his people. Many hours later, two half-drunken men left the little bar on the hillside.

The Blue Buick pulled up in front of our old house in Harmony Hall a little past five just as the evening began to cool down. It was Sunday December first - exactly three months after the famous Kendal Train Crash. The catastrophe was the news of the period; it was reported as the worst rail disaster in Jamaica's history, and the second worst rail disaster in the world at the time. According to a report in the Daily Gleaner: "On Sunday, September 1, 1957, hundreds of members of the Holy Name Society of St. Anne's Roman Catholic Church boarded a train at the Kingston Railway Station for an all day excursion to Montego Bay under the guidance of their pastor, the Reverend Father Charles Earle.

"Also on board were close to 100 known criminals, hooligans and pick-pockets. In all, the number of passengers totaled 1,600 an interesting feat given that the limit for each of the 12 cars was 80. The criminals were said to have caused such a ruckus during the trip that a priest declared that the wrath of God had surely descended on them.

"Unknown to him, that statement was prophetic. At around 11:30 p.m. on the train's return leg, as the two diesel engines and dozen wooden cars neared the sleeping town of Kendal, Manchester, three shrill whistle blasts signaled the journey's abrupt and tragic end. Within minutes, the train had picked up speed and derailed. Fragments of human bodies were strewn among scores of twisted metal. Close to 200 persons lost their lives, and 700 sustained injuries in what was described as the worst rail disaster in

Jamaica's history…"

Unfortunately, some of those 'fragments of human bodies' belonged to daddy's childhood friend, Danzo. As boys, Danzo and himself were very close friends, fighting each other, defending each other and just helping one another through good and bad times. Yep, he remembered, Danzo was like his own brother. They often ate out of the same plate and slept in the same bed.

Now, standing before his old house, daddy felt a sinking feeling of sadness, a tight dispiriting sense of foreboding, despite being pleased that he was home. He looked around and realized not much had changed. The familiar houses were still standing and he was certain the same people still lived there. He was brought back to the present when Roger came though the front door. His face lit up as he pumped daddy's hand.

"Lesta, Lesta. It so good fi see yuh. Mek me look pan yuh." He stepped back and surveyed daddy from head to toe. "Yuh nuh change at all eh? Excep' fi di gray 'air dem."

"Roger! Mi glad fi see yuh man. A yuh nuh change, nat even gray 'air."

"Come inside man. Come meet Pat." Roger pushed the door open, "Pat, Pat," he called noisily, "Lesta deh yah. 'Im come from Florida."

They entered the house as a tired looking forty-four-year old mulatto woman, looking more like sixty, timidly pushed her head through the half grubby cotton curtain separating the room from the kitchen.

"How yuh do Mass Lesta?" she asked, a halfhearted toothless smile appearing on her thin, reddish lips.

"Good, good, me aaright. Pleased fi meet yuh." Daddy peered at her closely; disappointment tightened his already taut stomach, his feelings disguised by the convivial smile on his face. She wasn't at all what he thought she'd be. Seven years older than Roger and two years older than himself, she appeared old and uncared for. Shriveled skin, toothless mouth, grimy fingernails and a sneaky shyness told him everything he wanted to know about her. Yet, she was Roger's choice, though they were never married. He made a silent promise not to interfere in his brother's business - even if invited.

"Yuh a go eat something, Sar?" He jerked to attention, abruptly awakened from his daydream.

"Yes, mi 'ungry," he confessed pulling a stool closer to the oily linoleum covered table.

"Yuh hear 'bout Danzo?" asked Roger, pulling another stool while Pat placed charcoal in the stove, lighting it, briefly filling the room with smoke.

"Tell me what 'appen."

"Di train crash and kill 'bout two 'undred a dem," volunteered Pat, putting the big, black Dutch pot of brown stewed chicken on the fire to heat.

"Dem seh dat di train was overfull, wid nearly two thousan' people, mos' a dem church people but a whole heap a criminal an pickpocket. Di Kingston bad boy dem cause it. Dem seh di criminal dem a switch on an' a switch off di light dem and a ramp wid di train equipment. Di ol' idiot dem walk up and down an' a trouble di church people dem. Dem drink, dem cuss an' mek a hole 'eap a noise." Roger fell quiet, shook his head sadly, then continued.

"Dem seh when di train get to a big, big corner near Kendal -

Yuh know Kendal near Mandeville?

Daddy bowed his head twice.

"Eh, Eh. Well as dem get inna di carner, di train pick up speed. It a go fas', fas' an' jus' jump off a di track. One by one, di coach dem derail, crashin' and mekin' a whole heap a noise, like a earthquake." He chuckled for the first time.

"Me hear seh di driver bawl out 'Wi dead now! Wi dead now!' an' blow di train whistle t'ree time before dem bang up, an' eight a di coach dem fly off a di track."

"Jeesas have is mercy," exclaimed Pat.

Daddy remained silent as Roger finished. Then a frown creased his forehead. "But what Danzo a do pon dat deh train?"

"Missa Lesta," Pat injected, "Mi hear seh, a Kingston Danzo did a look fi wuck..."

"Eh, heh," cut in Roger, but one a 'im frien' tell 'im 'bout wuck inna Montego Bay. Dat Sunday 'im go check a man from di company weh 'im frien' tell 'im 'bout in a Montego Bay and a come back when it 'appen..."

"But pan a Sunday?

"Well, a di 'otel business yuh nuh, an' from weh me hear, 'im fren tell 'im seh, a di bes' time fi see 'im.'

"Poor Danzo neva have a chance," said Pat grimly.

"One day Danzo deh ya, nex' day 'im gone," Roger sighed, a deep sorrow covering his heart like a mantle.

"Weh dem bury 'im?" My father wanted to know.

"So yuh nuh hear di story?" Roger queried, clearly delighted at being the first to tell the juicy tale.

"No."

"Dem carry mos' a 'im bady come bury same place yah. Behin' him faada house up di road."

"Weh yuh mean by mos' a 'im body?"

" 'Im mash up so bad, dem couldn' fin' 'im lef' han' an dem seh one a 'im foot crush up and dem cyaan fine some a 'im toe dem."

"Remember Lloyd?"

Daddy shook his head negatively.

"Yuh nuh memba Pinchie?" Pinchie, Lloyd? Up di road man. Beside Miss Issey?" Daddy thought about it; a frown on his face. Then he remembered and bowed his head vigorously.

"Well! Lloyd seh 'im see Danzo duppy all di while. 'Im seh, every time 'im see 'im, a one han' 'im have. Lloyd seh, di duppy always a look inna di bush dem, like 'im laas somet'ing. Everybady seh 'im lookin' fi 'im toe 'im, because up till dis day dem cyaan fin' di missing toe dem. People did seh a lie 'im a tell. But likkle by likkle odda people see 'im to. Always wid one han' a look fi 'im toe dem. All Mr. Sinclair seh 'im see 'im one night. Di Guzmore dem nuh like it, but nuff people seh dem see 'im."

"Poor Danzo," daddy said sadly. "Dem should look fi 'im body parts till dem fine dem. A hope dem no bury 'im toe an' han' wid no odder body. Because di two duppy dem will never res' until eeda (either of) dem solve di mix up or get some obeah man fi pacify di duppy dem and sen' dem to a resting place. We have to pray for our dear departed, so dat dem can rest in peace."

"Amen," said Uncle Roger and Pat simultaneously, "may Danzo an' all di odders rest in peace."

Daddy went to bed quite perplexed. Roger allowed him to use his old bed in the front room. He fell into a restless sleep after tossing for a while. He woke at about four in the wee morning hour, feeling an uncomfortable coldness. Getting out of bed daddy closed the window, light from the moon seeped through the window illuminating one side of his bed. He was about to slip under the covers, when he noticed the opposite side of the bed sunken as if someone was resting there. Suddenly, the room felt deadly cold and daddy knew there was someone in the room apart from him.

Daddy is a man of strong Godly conviction but the unexpectedness startled him. He closed his eyes and whispered a prayer. When he opened them again, the bed was back to normal but the squeak behind him made him glance over his shoulder, the rocking chair in the corner tipped forward then rocked as if someone was sitting and rocking it. Daddy pretended not to notice, pulled the cover to his neck, and went to sleep. Sleep did not come easily, the spirit jerked the bed, rocked articles, and made a general raucous but daddy remained stock-still until he fell asleep.

My father made no mention of the experience to anyone and was not disturbed for the next five nights. He filled his days by visiting friends all over Harmony Hall. He went to the Guzmore's house twice without seeing anyone. On the third day, a man tending to the yard told him the family had gone to Kingston for the week and would be back Saturday. Sunday after church, daddy visited the Guzmore family again. They were as happy to see him as he was to see them. They invited him to stay for dinner, which he did.

Amy Guzmore, Danzo's wife, and his sister Doreen, prepared a delicious dinner of curried goat and rice and peas. Daddy met Danzo's seven-year-old son Eric for the first time. He was a shy but bright little fellow and daddy liked him immediately saying the lad reminded him of Danzo when he was a boy. After dinner, Eric went about his business leaving the grown ups to socialize. Daddy told them about our shop and his story-telling occupation. They were thirsty for knowledge about Florida and he filled them in wherever he could.

Then daddy asked them about Danzo and the accident. They confirmed Roger's account of the accident and Danzo's involvement. Then Daddy took a deep breath and asked: "Tell mi, Danzo duppy ever bodder any a yuh?"

"No sah," chorused the women.

"But people seh dem see 'im a search fi 'im toe dem. How dem know seh a 'im toe 'im a look fa God He knows," said Amy indignantly.

"So unno nuh believe dem?"

"No sah. Yuh know Minny Hall people dem, dem jus' a look somet'ing fi talk 'bout."

"A true yuh a talk. But mek me tell yuh somet'ing. Las' Sunday night, firs' night when mi come back, Danzo was in di room." They were silent, staring at him intently. The ladies knew this was not idle talk.

" 'Im mus be glad fi see me because di whole night 'im stay in a di room. At firs', mi was frighten' because mi neva know seh a 'im, but as soon as me realize a who mi jus' go sleep."

"How yuh know seh a Danzo?" asked Amy.

Daddy smiled, "Because Danzo always a play wid the ol' rocking chair in a di bedroom. From wi a boy, mi faada use to seh Danzo love da chair more dan anybody else. Daddy looked at them fixedly, "yuh know how ol' dat chair is?"

"Mi know it older dan me because me born come see it," said Danzo's sister.

"Eh, eh. It 'bout fifty 'ears old or more. Sunday night, di duppy move from di bed to di chair. It rock di chair back and forth jus' like Danzo used to. An' a inna it the duppy sleep whole night." Daddy experienced an intense desire to convince the ladies it was Danzo and he wanted more than anything else to persuade them that his duppy needed to be put to rest, peacefully.

Amy bowed her head to hide the tears emerging from her eyes and muttered, "A miss 'im so much Lester, mi wish me did dead wid 'im."

"Never mind mi dear," he hushed her tenderly but she could not speak for a while, stifling sobs as emotions overwhelmed her. Doreen sat rigidly, stone-faced saying not a word.

After a long interval of silence, Doreen spoke a bit crisply. "Mi know seh a him to. To tell di trut', every now an' den mi feel 'im around me. Him nuh trouble me but 'im mek me know seh 'im nah rest well. Lester, yuh a 'im good, good fren, wha' we mus' do?"

"Well," daddy spoke very carefully, "we mus' fin' what 'im a search for or ask somebody fi talk to 'im an' mek 'im know seh everything alright an' 'im mus' go rest."

"We cyaan find 'im han' or toe dem cause dem mash up so badly an' mix up wid odders, we wouldn't know which a fi him." Amy stated with chilling frankness.

"Derefore, we mus' talk to di bes' obeah man inna di distric' an' pay 'im fi 'elp we."

"But we nuh have nuh money Lester," cried Amy.

"No worry, me will pay fi it," said Daddy earnestly.

The atmosphere became lighter as they sat and discussed the issue. They decided to seek the services of Bokorta Preval, the obeah man from Haiti. Old man Bokorta had been a pillar of support, in the district, for over seven years now, helping many get rid of troublesome duppies, curses, and even sicknesses which medical doctors couldn't heal.

The people in Highgate believed in Bredda Bokorta although this was not always so. He had migrated from Haiti as a voodoo priest and local

black magic man. But the people of Highgate did not like strangers - especially from another country- telling them about black magic, obeah or any
other form of necromantic practice. After all, Highgate had the best obeah
men in the country, two of them - except, of course, Mass Tomassa, the old
Obeah man who lived in the hills of St. Thomas. Everyone said he is the
best, and everyone believed the old man would live forever. But one of
Highgate's obeah men died and Bredda Bokorta proved himself to be good
when he healed Jenny, the little girl down the road who was hit by a bicy-
cle and was certain to die. The Haitian gained their confidence and, until
this day, most of Highgate people went to him.

My father and the Guzmores agreed to see Bredda Bokorta the following Saturday evening. They met him at his house and he led the three of
them to his temple.

"Mi know why yuh come." He said flatly. "Is full time somebody do
somet'ing 'bout di poor man. But it gwine cos' yuh."

They entered the small building he called his temple. It looked just like
a tiny church with two benches on either side of the aisle leading to a platform with a rostrum. It was here the similarity to a church disappeared.
Bones were scattered all over the platform. A red, white and blue silken
cloth covered the pulpit and in the corners were many candles on tall
wooden stands. High on a stick in the centre, hung an artificial human
skull, which most people believe was real. Bredda Bokorta lifted an open
bible from the rostrum and told them to sit.

"Ayza, the protector..." he began, just as Daddy held up his hand.

"Bredda Bokorta, yuh don't know me, but I was a good friend a'
Danzo..."

"Yes, yes mi know who yuh be."

"Ok, but mek wi discuss how much it a go cost before..."

"No mind dat we have to call pan di spirit firs'."

"Ok."

And with that Bredda Bokorta carried out a two-minute prayer ritual.
When he was finished, he said to his visitors: "The cost is seven pounds fi
put poor brother Danzo to rest. I see him a couple times an' him in torment.
We mus' release him. Normally, me charge ten pounds but mi want to help,
so mi take off three pounds."

Seven pounds was a lot of money. Daddy thought it would cost about
five pounds but he didn't complain. He stretched out his hand with a five-
pound note and two single pounds. The money disappeared as fast as it

appeared while Bredda Bokorta lit the candles.

"Yuh all have to leave me now before the Baron Samedi, the guardian of the grave, appear. Tonight for sure, brother Danzo will be at rest. Come back one fortnight from now and mi will confirm everything."

They left him humming and chanting, assured everything would be ok. The fortnight would fall on the Saturday and daddy was scheduled to return home. The threesome agreed he did not have to be there as the women could take care of everything. They thanked him for his generosity and went their ways.

Daddy spent the days visiting friends and telling them about America. Many wanted to know if he could help them get a visa to travel. It was burdensome telling them he couldn't help especially since traveling was so expensive, but as usual, daddy was honest and said he couldn't. He gave away most of the money he traveled with, spending some to buy drinks, mostly alcohol, for friends and strangers in bars he visited. He was careful to keep enough for his return trip.

Daddy planned to take the bus from Highgate to Kingston and a cab from the terminus to the airport. This way he had more money to spend with his friends instead of paying taxi fare from Highgate to Kingston. The day before daddy was to leave, he, Roger, and friends were having a good time in Tracey's bar, close to Bredda Bokorta's house, when the Haitian guzzu man appeared outside beckoning to daddy to come speak with him.

"Mi have a message from Danzo for you."

"What?"

"No," he said shaking his head, "you have to come with me."

Daddy looked perplexed.

"Don't worry it not costing you anything."

They walked to the temple. Bredda Bokorta told Daddy to sit while he went to his house. When he returned, he carried two small cups without handles, a brown steaming hot liquid filled them to the brim.

He gave daddy one cup and sipped from the other, motioning him to drink. The liquid was hot and bitter to the taste but it wasn't loathsome. They drank without saying a word until the containers were empty.

"How do you feel?" the Haitian asked.

Daddy began to answer but his lips felt numb, like when dentist had pumped cocaine in it, his head twirled and his brain began to float. Daddy felt mindless, unable to focus. He realized he couldn't answer, just couldn't form any words. Then a cool breeze enveloped his head and filled the room without causing a flicker to the candles.

The Obeah man lit two other candles, closely watching my father, and then he covered them with the now empty cups. A red-hot ball of fire rose from under each cup and circled the room as my father sat watching helplessly.

"Danzo, Danzo, come to us Danzo," he heard the obeah man chanting, "we await your presence Danzo." All of a sudden both balls of fire clashed together over the rostrum and a massive cloud of smoke enveloped the whole room. Then it became cold, real cold. A strong wind entered from an unopened window and daddy could no longer see. He struggled to stand but his feet fell into emptiness. It was then he realized he was floating, floating high in the skies. As he floated, he regained his sight only to realize he had no wings, just the ability to soar. So he glided easily over the green hills of St. Mary on his way to an unknown destination. Then he saw it, the narrow, winding, precipitous, junction road leading to Kingston. And there it was, the bus he planned to travel on the next day.

The driver pushed the gas pedal hard as the vehicle careened around corner after corner. The passengers seem to be having a great time, everyone laughing and leaning on each other as the bus tilted on its axel around the sharp bends.

Daddy tried to pull himself away from the inevitable but couldn't. He closed his eyes and opened them again just as the bus hit the embankment and toppled over the precipice, screams thundering up to the heavens. He watched helplessly as bodies smashed against metal and the bus came to rest on a rocky dirt ledge just short of the bottom where the Wag Waters awaited. He floated down towards the wreck and saw it as clearly as in life, corpse after corpse laid out on the side of the precipice, looking like bundles of dirty clothes.

My father closed his eyes again and found himself back in the temple; the Haitian sat quietly watching him.

"Danzo told you." It was a statement, not a question.

"Yes," daddy confessed, "it was horrible, horrible mi seh. We mus' stop di bus."

"You can't my friend. You can't. Only thing is yuh mustn' take that bus tomorrow. Take a taxi or wait until another day."

"But we mus' do somet'ing fi help dem."

"Help them? How? What you going to tell them? That Danzo tell you? No one would believe you. Anyway, where you going to find dem to tell them? The bus comes from way up Guy's Hill. You won't see them before tomorrow morning."

"Then, mek wi warn dem tomorrow."

"They wouldn't listen to you and wouldn't believe a word you say. And you don't have the time if you are going to take a taxi anyway. Rememba you have a plane to catch."

Daddy agreed there was nothing he could do except pray and stop anyone he knew would take the bus. But there was no one he knew taking the bus, so all he did was pray. He prayed just before he fell asleep and saw Danzo in a dream. Danzo was happy, dressed in full white. He smiled as he approached Daddy.

"Thanks," he said beaming, "we will meet again but for now I have to rest."

Daddy looked quizzically not understanding why he was thanking him. Danzo spoke again, "I can rest now because of your kindness. Thanks my friend, and do not worry about the people on the bus, only a few will perish. Just don't take the bus and say hello to your family for me." Before he could respond, Danzo was gone and he sat up wide-awake, the room peaceful and calm.

My father awoke much earlier than originally planned and walked to Highgate where he hired the only taxi in town. The driver arrived with terrible news, the bus to Kingston had crashed around the Junction road killing three people and injuring over twenty. Daddy said not a word. Sadness engulfed him as he said goodbye to his brother and friends. He was certain it was the last time he would see them and they knew it too. He promised to write and drove off noticing the tears in Roger's and Pat's eyes. After all, he had come to like Pat, even love her, because she was so kind and good to his brother. He would remember Danzo for the rest of his life.

The taxi driver wanted to stop where the crowd gathered around the scene of the accident but daddy wanted to see none of it, he already knew how the entire area looked. He ordered him to drive on, arriving at the airport with over two hours to spare. He paid the man, checked in and bought himself a drink at the bar. Six hours later mama met him at the airport and they drove home together, his Jamaican story bursting out in torrents.

Chapter 6

*D*awn Cretin was thirteen when she first came to Belle Glade
School. Her flat coffee brown face was attractive in a funny kind
of way. Maybe it was her thin athletic ballet dancer body, or her
unusually small slant eyes like that of people from the Orient, or maybe it
was the manner she carried herself; head in the air, shoulders erect as if she
was royalty. I couldn't quite tell what it was about her, but she certainly
attracted attention. Tom liked her even though she was half black, half East
Indian despite his constant declaration that he didn't like the local girls. I
always thought Tom was crazy. How could an African American boy not
like local African American girls? I couldn't figure it out, but that was Tom.
He explained that it was not because he didn't like local black girls but he
didn't like local American black girls. His excuse for liking this particular
girl was that Dawn is Jamaican and therefore different from what he called
local Yankees, a word he picked up from his father - *The Duke.*

I wasn't interested in girls; all my focus was on becoming a storyteller
like my father. School meant being with my friends and trying to remember poems, solving math problems, reading and such burdensome efforts
while my spare time was filled with playing gig and yoyo, flying kites,
fishing, and such fun activities. I had enough problems trying to cope with
the pressure from mama and Miss McDonald (my teacher) to study hard
and become some Doctor or Lawyer or accountant, or enter some other
profession that I wasn't interested in. Getting involved with girls would
only compound my problems plus, at that time of my life, I just wasn't
interested.

Dawn hated Tom and all his friends, which included me, but as I said
it did not matter to me at all. She took great pleasure in calling him Tom-
Du knowing the meaning of the nickname. He abhorred it but Dawn was
the one person who could use that name without a fight and she did - often

enough. It didn't take Tom long to realize her dislike was real. He learnt to stay away from her.

Years later, while we were in our final year in Belle Glade School, a friend called me to watch the senior girls going through their Physical Education class. By then, I had certainly learnt to appreciate the importance of girls, having dropped some of my other fun activities. The girls were neatly dressed in navy-blue shorts and sky-blue tops and the shorts were tight and skimpy hugging their upper thighs like a hand in a glove. They all looked neat, smart and pretty. As we watched my friend quietly asked, "Cecil, who has the best legs in the group?"

I knew the answer before he asked.

"Dawn," I said, "Dawn Cretin."

"Mmmmm Hmmm," he said, deeply taken up with the picture of loveliness, jumping up and down on coffee coloured, flawlessly shaped legs. It was then that I knew. I must do something. At least to say hello to her.

While Tom was at Belle Glade School, I was one of the popular guys but after he left, I had to pretend to be 'with it', a part of the 'in crowd'. The guys believed I was sharp with the girls although I really was shy and terrified to even approach them. My only interest was telling duppy and other thrilling stories about Jamaica. And, since some of the girls loved to hear my stories, I could always fool the crowd with the façade of popularity. Yes! I was alive and kicking at story time but dead as a doorknob when it came to speaking to girls. Today though, I was determined to speak to the one girl who hated my guts.

A week passed and, still, I did not have the nerve to approach Dawn. Then, one lunch period, I saw her sitting alone under a tree. With my heart in my mouth, I walked steadily towards her. She saw me coming and looked at me quizzically.

"Hello," I said, hoping the trembling in my voice wasn't detected.

"Hello Mr. Storyteller." I didn't know if she said it with a smile or a reprimand but I now realized she knew who I was. I flopped down beside her, all the time thinking; hell, she's never been to one of my storytelling sessions.

"You're Dawn! Right?"

"Of course I'm Dawn and you are Cecil Jenkins. Aren't you?" Her snappy words took me aback and I chided myself for the bad start.

"Look Dawn," I said stupidly, "we guys were watching you girls during PE and voted you the best legs of all the girls."

"What?" she snapped.

Oh God! I thought, what a fool, damn, damn fool. Can't I ever do something right - for once?

"You know Cecil Jenkins," I heard her saying, "you are a lame excuse for a storyteller."

I dared to look her in the eyes then and was surprised to see kindness instead of hostility. A little smile danced around her soft lips and her eyes twinkled with mischief. Suddenly, it seemed I had not really lost her but I had to be careful.

"Serious though Dawn, you are really very nice and I like you."

"You like me or my legs? Cecil Jenkins?" She continued to use my full name in that strong, domineering, standoffish manner that kept me off balance.

"Both," I said, "I like both you and your legs."

"Ok," she said dismissively.

I stood, smiled at her, and said bravely (to this day, I don't know where I got the mettle), "I'll be asking you out soon Dawn Cretin," and walked away without looking back.

It wasn't long before I did ask her out and though I was shaking as usual, something told me she would say yes and she did. We watched a comedy at the local theatre. It was a very funny movie, which we both enjoyed enormously. After that, we decided to 'go steady' - she was my girlfriend and I was her boyfriend.

I was seventeen and Dawn was sixteen during the fall when daddy went to Jamaica. She had gone back to spend the holidays with her parents in New York. I did agree with mama that I would go to winter camp in New York, primarily because Dawn was there and we planned to meet at the first opportunity that arose. No way on earth, would I swap anything for this trip to New York. She told me about fun filled days playing in pure white snow and I looked forward to seeing some snow for the first time.

It really did snow in New York that year and I had a glorious time. Because we were young adults, our camp director did not place the strict limits they usually do with younger kids. We had the opportunity to visit relatives and friends as long as we told the director where we were going and whom we were going to, as well as producing a letter of invitation from our hosts. Dawn pressed her mother to provide the letter for me and I spent two weekends with the Cretins. It was the most memorable trip in my entire life.

When I returned, daddy was back from Jamaica and I learned of his extraordinary experience there. He planned his first story telling Saturday for the first Saturday of February. We were back in school for our last semester before college. I invited Dawn to daddy's storytelling session and she accepted, although she made it clear she was not very fond of duppy stories.

She arrived at our house on time and I introduced her to my parents as my school friend. Mama wanted to know why she had not met her before but I sidestepped the question to serve Dawn some of our delicious fruit drink. We settled outside as usual to listen to daddy. He was getting on in age but very rarely missed a planned first Saturday, especially after advertising his upcoming story. For two weeks, daddy made it known he was going to do something he had never done before, it was to tell a true story about his own experience; an involvement with a duppy bird.

The group was very large; it must have been the largest we had ever had. Massa Grey, the oldest sharecropper in Florida, visited us for story time. A man of many stories himself, Mass Joe said he longed to hear one of Daddy's stories. He was the first farm worker out of Highgate to come to Florida and many Jamaicans, including daddy, owed much to this skinny, shriveled old man. He guided them, protected them, fed them when they were hungry, and negotiated for them when they were being underpaid.

Yes, we all knew Old Massa Grey was a teacher and friend to all African Americans, Jamaican Americans, and all folks who he thought were kind and good and he was more than welcome at our home.

In honour of Massa Grey's presence, daddy asked him to tell one of his stories.

"Nah," he said, "Lester, yuh a di story tella. Me ongle come fi listen."

But Daddy insisted.

"Even a short one Massa Grey, everyone will love to hear it."

We all clapped and shouted our encouragement.

"Alright, alright," he said, "dis is one of mi favourite story. I been hearing it from me was a bwoy. Me don't know if a true or not but mi t'ink it funny."

The old man forced himself up using his cane for balance. Shakily, and with the practice of a seasoned storyteller he ambled towards the stairs, his cigar puffing made his mouth twitch as he spoke.

"As far as me can rememba, me faada first tell me dis story. It happen a long time ago, before him pass on. God bless him soul."

Every eye followed him as he moved toward the stairs then he stopped, shook his cane in the air, pointed it at the crowd and asked.

"Anyone a h'unno love fi walk a night?"

A light murmur passed among the crowd, but no one exactly answered.

"Well," he continued, "afta unno hear dis story, which I t'ink maybe true, unno won't want fi walk a night no more."

By this time Massa Grey reached the steps and held out his hands to Daddy; that's when I realized, for the first time, my father was really getting old. He struggled to stand, extended his hands and smiled. I noticed the strings in his neck, the boniness of his hand and the strain of his composure. But daddy was every bit of an actor, as he was a storyteller. He lifted old Massa Grey's left hand with his right and exclaimed, "Mek wi welcome one of di bes' man in di whole of Belle Glade -Massa Grey".

The crowd cheered and daddy sat down laboriously, an action missed neither by my mother nor me.

As my father took his seat, the old sharecropper smiled at the crowd and began his story.

Tampi and The Duppy

In the thirties, back home in Harmony Hall there lived a man with two sons. One of them was a good boy but the other was very bad and loved to walk late at nights. I don't remember the good boy's name but his bad brother's name was Tampi. As I said before, Tampi loved to walk late at nights although his father warned him about the duppies in the district. One night, after they came from church, Tampi decided to look for a girl, down the road, named Sandra Peat. Now, in those days, there was a deep curve, in the road, with a big cotton tree right in the curve. Everyone knew heaps of duppies lived in the cotton tree and the curve was so deep, we used to call *Steel Curve.*

I tell you, even big men wouldn't walk alone at night around Steel Curve but Tampi didn't care, though the boy would soon learn to care. Well, as Tampi reach' the curve, he saw a man. At first, he thought he recognized him but as he got closer he realized it was a stranger. He went up to the man with a cigarette in his fingers. The boy stabbing the cigarette in his mouth approached the man and asked.

"Gimme a light nuh."

The stranger turned to him and chuckled. The snicker was so frosty that Tampi felt a chill run down his spine. He looked up into the man's face and couldn't believe his eyes. The man had long red teeth, and eyes like fire blazing in the dark night. As Tampi stared, the duppy gashed his teeth. Realization hit the boy like a brick; he took to his heels. He ran so fast, in his mind, he was certain not even the duppy could follow him. The boy didn't stop until he saw company before him.

Now, Tampi was still a little distance from home and was glad to see a real human being who he could talk to and walk with as company to his house. Blowing like a mule, he caught up to the man and began telling him how unfortunately he saw a horrible duppy up by *Steel Curve.* He told the man the duppy had the largest, reddest teeth he had ever seen and his eyes were like the living fire.

The man turned to him, grinned his teeth, and asked, "Teet' like these, longa than these?"

Man, Tampi took to his heels again and ran like a mad man for his house. Needless to say he was the fastest man in Jamaica that night. His heart was beating faster and faster and his only prayer was not to meet another stranger before he got home. Fortunately, he did not meet anyone, live man or duppy, before he reached the safety of his house.

In the days that followed, no one could believe Tampi could change so much. He learnt his lesson well and became a good boy. He never walked alone late at night ever again.

The entire group cracked up with laughter although some of us, especially the younger ones, were a little shaken. Some people wanted to know if it really happened.

"One t'ing I know is," Massa Grey responded, "no one in Minny Hall (that's what dem used to call Harmony Hall in those days) ever walk alone, round Steel Curve, once dusk come down."

Slowly, the old man walked back to his seat, an easy sense of satisfaction affecting his every step. Daddy pulled himself up and started clapping. Everyone stood and cheered. It was the first standing ovation since our storytelling began.

After the cheering subsided, Old Massa Grey thanked us and, directing his attention to daddy, made his request.

"Lester," he said, "mi travel a far way fi listen to one of yuh story. It might be di las' story me hear. So Lester, mek wi hear what happen to yuh and di bird."

My father smiled weakly and slowly shook his head.

"Yes mi friends, I reserve one of mi bes' story fi yuh."

Little did we know, my daddy was fast approaching the end of his storytelling days. Daddy's voice rang strong and sure as he told the story of one of his own experience when he was just a lad. I had heard this story before, but it was a long time ago while we lived in Jamaica. He never told any story about himself, since coming to America, although back home he told us about many of his own encounters with the dreaded duppy.

I couldn't help but smile as he began and then I realized he noticed my joy, because he shook his head in an ever so subtle bow, smiled at me, a twinkle in his eyes.

Now, years later, I realize my Daddy was passing storytelling on to me and sadness filled my heart because I did not realize it then. I could have hugged him, I could have kissed him, I could have told him how happy he made me all my life by skillfully, ever so skillfully, telling his tales of duppy encounters in Highgate, St. Mary. But I didn't know, I didn't tell him, I didn't hug him and, that night he told his greatest story ever.

Daddy's habit was to sit comfortably and begin his story. When it was warranted, he'd stand and act through a scene. Today, he sat evenly on the steps, where he always sat. The words flowed effortlessly from his yielding lips, sometimes strong, sometimes weak, sometimes loud, sometimes soft. Sometimes the earth seemed to shake as he spoke, bringing us into his world. Everyone there felt the impact of his duppy tale as fear, sadness, delight and enchantment mixed emotions in our souls. After all, for the first time, daddy was telling a story about himself. It was the latest he had ever started a story; the clock struck nine as he spoke about the Duppy Bird.

Duppy Bird

I was terribly afraid of the lady next door. She was pregnant and had a big stomach that made it difficult for her to walk. The big belly lady did not like children and was always cursing Mr. Bredda who, they say, was the father of her child. Mr. Bredda was a nice man. He sometimes gave me a ride on the country bus he drove from Annotto Bay to Port Maria. One day, he did not turn up for work and another man began to drive the bus. Mr. Bredda was never seen again, in Highgate; although rumour had it he was driving a chi-chi bus in Kingston. Since then, the lady next door got even worse, cussing under her breath and complaining about feeling sick.

My Aunty Nerissa owned the house next door and rented the front apartment to the pregnant lady. The lady's name was Martha Cummings but we all called her Miss Mana, which she liked. The only person Miss Mana really liked was my mother, but my mother died when I was five years old. She did not like my cousin Claudette who came to help father take care of us. Though Claudette was eight years older than me, we lived like close friends, playing cards and ludo till late at nights. On this bright Monday morning, Claudette was angry with me because I did not want to go next door. I was afraid of Mana.

"Go for di money nuh Lester,!" she screamed at me.

"But Claudette, yuh go for it nuh," I begged.

"Mi have to bathe yuh sista and get her ready fi school. Den mi have to fix di breakfast. Gwaan nuh man."

There was no way out and, so, I slowly walked towards my Aunty's house. Just as I figured, Ms. Mana was sitting on the doorsteps, her dress lapped between her legs. Her big belly pushed out in front of her. She was eating a ripe banana, stuffing half of it in her mouth at one time. The banana expanded her jaws and she chewed with vigour. I wondered why Ms. Mana always had a big brown comb tucked in her graying hair. The only time she smiled was when she was speaking of her great grandfather, who, she said, came here from India. She always boasted that she got her nice, curly hair from him.

"Mawnin' Miss Mana," I said, softly stepping by her.

"Come here bwoy." She could hardly speak with the banana occupying her mouth.

"Yuh nuh have nuh mannas? Yuh couldn' say mawnin' dawg?"

"But mi say mawnin', Miss Mana," I answered meekly, realizing she had not heard my greeting.

"Da's why mi nuh like pickney yuh nuh. Mi a look straight pan yuh and yuh neva say a word. Yuh a call mi lia'd pickney?"

"No Miss Mana." I said, running towards my Aunty's apartment.

"Yuh gwaan bwoy."

I barely heard her words as I dashed through the door.

My Aunty was waiting for me, money in her outstretched hand. She noticed the dread in my eyes and hugged me.

"What's di matta Lester?"

"Nothing Aunty," I lied, not wanting her to know I was afraid of Mana.

"Well son, yuh late fi school already, so run an' buy di bread," she paused, "Come back quick yuh hear?"

"Yes Aunty," I replied, moving towards the door, my stomach in a knot thinking about Mana. But she was no longer sitting outside.

The following day, at four, I came home from school. A crowd was gathered at our gate and I learnt Miss Mana was taken to the hospital because she had fallen and was bleeding. By the next morning, both Miss Mana and the baby died. They were buried behind our house under the big star apple tree, beside the gully. And that was the beginning of my nightmare.

One early Sunday morning, not long after the funeral, my father's voice awoke me; he was shouting.

"What the hell yuh mean by coming to my house so early this Sunday morning, eh?"

"Well! I have been trying for the past two months to get in touch with you but you were never around. They tell me you were out of town. I need the mortgage - now!" bellowed a voice I recognized. It was Mr. Forrester, the banker. Daddy and Mr. Forrester were good friends but of late they have not been seeing eye-to-eye. Daddy had lost his job and was doing part-time work, which wasn't paying well, so he couldn't afford the mortgage.

"Yuh expect me to have eighty pounds in the house on a Sunday morning?"

"Ok, ok, Benjy, I will give you until the end of the month to come up with the money. Either you give me the full amount or be out of here by the end of the month."

The burly banker stormed out of the house and was gone. Two weeks later my father called us in the living room and gave us the news.

"We goin' to live in yuh Aunty's house next door," he declared.

"Wha' Daddy? In di house weh Miss Mana used to live?"

He saw the shock, the terror on my face.

"Yes son, I can't pay for dis house no more. I have to sell it."

"But Daddy…"

"Son, afta I sell it an' pay them, I will soon have enough money to buy another. Believe mi son we gwine buy a better one."

I did not want a better house. I liked this house more than any other, plus I was petrified by the thought of living in the house where Miss Mana died. But I couldn't tell Dad.

"Yes Daddy," I said innocently.

A week later we moved in.

The place seemed tiny compared to our much larger house. My sister's bed and mine were placed at opposite ends of the same room. Daddy occupied the front room and Claudette stayed in the small room between Daddy's and ours. There was a passage between our apartment and Aunty's. Her apartment was around the back, furthest away from the road.

For the first two weeks, every night, I dreamt something about Miss Mana. During those weeks, I begged my father not to leave us alone. He enjoyed playing poker (I suspect that's where some of the mortgage went) and didn't get home until early morning most weekends. But he knew I was afraid and gave up the practice for a while. The weeks turned into months and I went back to my regular routine. I forgot about Miss Mana and Daddy resumed his weekend poker games.

One of my favorite past time was shooting birds. My friends thought I was a novice at it but they respected my ability to make a good slingshot. I would be rich today if the friends I had paid me for each slingshot I made for them. I still remember Glen owed me, at least, a shilling for the three slingshots I made for him; he never gave me a penny although I furnished all the material.

One Saturday morning, after the rain subsided, I saw an Antspick bird on a mango tree, a few feet away from the veranda. I grabbed my sling-shot and crept close enough to get a good shot. I let the stone go and it hit the bird squarely on the wing. It fluttered to the ground and I jubilantly ran to pick it up. As I bent to touch the bird, it bounced against my hands and flew away. After the incident, strange things began to happen.

I went to bed late one Saturday night. Daddy was out playing poker so Claudette, my sister and I played 'rummy' and 'three cards pretty' until nearly eleven o'clock. Normally, when Claudette heard my father walking up the steps towards the house she'd peek through the curtains to make certain it was him, then open the door to let him in. At four thirty that morning, she heard the familiar footsteps. She turned on the outside light, pulled away the curtain and looked outside but did not see anyone. As she turned off the light, the footsteps sounded louder coming up the stairs. She turned on the light and looked again, the sound ceased and again there was no one to be seen - anywhere.

My sister and I were sound asleep in our room with the lights on. We were unaware of the terror that gripped Claudette as she dove into the bed pulling the cover over her head. After a moment, she heard three sharp knocks on the door. That definitely sounded like Daddy, she thought, pulling away the cover, jumping out of bed and opening the door. There before her was the boniest woman she had ever seen. Her entire body looked like a skeleton and her eyes were sunken deep into her head. The woman seemed to float as she began a gyrating dance with outstretched arms as if wanting to hold Claudette. As she danced, her waist moving forward ever so slowly, Claudette screamed and ran into our room. She grabbed my sister and pulled her into my bed screaming incessantly.

I awoke with Claudette jumping on my bed and the house in total darkness.

"Lawd Jesas Chris', Help! Help!" Claudette shouted.

Immediately, the light came on in our room. That's when I remembered I left it on before going to sleep. By this time, all three of us were terrified; we were fully aware, hands that were not human had switched on the lights. Then I saw it; a little Antspick flew from our room through the open window.

Claudette continued to shout, "Help! Help! Aunt Nerissa help. Aunt Nerissa, yuh hear mi, Jesas help!"

We barely heard my Aunt's voice, "Is who dat?"

"Is me Claudette, Aunt Nerissa, A mi. Help!"

"Come mi chile. Bring di children dem come."

We hugged Claudette as she rushed out the back door, through the passage to Aunty's apartment where she stood at the door waiting for us. Once into the house, Claudette started to babble. The words sounded slurred, she could hardly speak.

"Shhhhhh! Don't say a word. Drink dis," said Aunty handing Claudette a glass with some brownish fluid.

Claudette drank long and deep sucking up every drop of the liquid. When she was finished, she began to cry. Her words were clearer and she was more composed but Aunty forbid her to talk.

"Wait until morning," she said, "I know somet'ing terrible happen. I been feeling it all night and know evil was around. Go to bed now, we will talk tomorrow."

She ushered us into the guest room where we slept for the night.

Next morning, Claudette told us about the skeleton lady and how she reached for her as she danced. I told them about the Antspick bird I'd seen flying through the window, only to find out, I was the only one who had seen it. Aunty looked at me and shook her head knowingly.

"Dat bird was a duppy bird," she said, "an' I know who it is. But don't worry."

"Is who Aunty?" I probed, shivering knowingly.

"Is a evil bird mi bwoy. It need to go res'."

"But it might come back?" I prodded.

"Don't worry son, me will mek sure nuh harm don' come to none a yuh."

That was not to be.

During the following days, the rain fell steadily. St. Mary is a rainy parish and, in Highgate, rain sometimes falls for weeks. The town is located on a hill, causing the water to run off very fast. Our house was located at the foot of a steep grade. There were eight concrete steps leading to the veranda and the other section of the house was built high, at least five feet. The house was so high it was impossible for a frog to jump up the stairs to the veranda and yet, almost every night, my father found a frog on the veranda or in the dining room. He'd get a brown paper bag, placed it over the frog and throw it outside. He never killed any and preferred not to talk about it.

One day, my Aunty, who is renowned for her powers with evil spirits, told my father to call her when he found another frog. He did so the very next day. Within an hour she came with some yellowish brown liquid in a bottle. After securing us in our room (my sister and I could only hear her speaking in loud tones), she ordered the frog to leave, sprinkling the liquid over it and in the four corners of the room. She spoke in a language we had never heard before, or since then, commanding the frog never to enter our dwelling again. Aunty called the Lord's name three times and left. No frog ever entered our house again.

For weeks, nothing unusual happened. Then, one night, I went to bed and fell in a deep sleep. I knew nothing until seven o'clock the next morning when I awoke in Dr. Derider's office, an injection needle in my bottom. I opened my eyes to see the very worried face of my father staring down at me.

"Thank di Lord," he said, "yuh wake up."

He hugged me and kissed me while the doctor looked on.

"How do you feel son," the doctor asked.

"Fine," I said, looking around trying to figure what had happened.

It was not until three days after the incident that Claudette told me what had happened. Neither my father nor my Aunty would talk about it - everyone kept a tight lip. It is believed three days must pass after a Duppy is seen before it is safe to talk about the incident.

On the night of the incident, Claudette had gone to bed and had a dream. In the dream, she was sitting on the veranda and saw Martha Cummings coming from my bedroom (Mana's old bedroom). Claudette rose to confront Mana, conscious that she was about to face a duppy.

"Wha' yuh doin' inna di pickney dem room?"

"Dis ya room a mine," croaked the ghost.

"Yours?" Claudette sneered, "but yuh nuh dead?"

At the use of the word dead, Duppy Mana got furious. "Yuh will see a who dead. Yuh will see."

"Leave an' don't come back yah, rotten belly 'oman, don't come back."

The duppy, backing away, shrieked: "Dat bwoy Lester shot mi. Mi a go lick him back. Tell im fi 'top use slingshot."

"Yuh cyaan do 'im nutten. Yuh cyaan touch 'im, rotten belly. Go weh rotten belly 'oman!" Claudette screamed, rubbing her stomach vigorously with her left hand.

She knew duppies hated being called 'rotten belly' as their bodies hurt and their stomach churned with nausea and wooziness if, you rub your stomach energetically with your left hand while calling them rotten belly. Duppy Mana's eyes turned backwards in her head, her skin withered, and her once beautiful hair turned white and orange-green. She was in pain but struggled to have the last word before she left.

"Yuh will seeeeeeee. Yeeeees! Yuh will seeeeeeeeeee."

The duppy vanished and Claudette awoke with a jolt, sweat pouring down her face. Fear gripped the eighteen-year-old; she looked around assuring herself it was only a dream. She glanced at her bedside clock; it was five thirty in the morning -almost daylight.

Suddenly, the room felt cold like a morgue and the overpowering smell of dead flesh hit her nearly causing her to retch. She held back the vomit and, covering her nose dashed into our room.

"Lawd Jesas," she screamed jumping on my bed.

She saw me then and became terrified. My eyes were closed and thick white froth spewed from my lips. Claudette grabbed me and began to shake me vigorously. My eyes opened for a second. It had a glazed look and was far too red to be normal. She ran to my father's room.

"Uncle Benjy! Uncle Benjy!" she shouted, her small hands waving wildly in the air, "Come, come now, Lester a go dead."

"What?" my father thunderous voice echoed his unbelief. He shot from the bed and dashed after Claudette to my room. My sister was awake, now sitting in bed crying her head off. My father lifted me in his arms and shook my head over and over while Claudette kept wiping the continuously flowing froth from my mouth.

"Don't die Lester, please don't die," my father cried, showing more emotions than he ever did in all his life. He carried me to the veranda still unconscious and foaming at the mouth.

"Get a taxi," he shouted but Claudette had already gone to seek help from the Britons next door. Without hesitation, Mr. Briton donned his working clothes, jumped in his car, started it and we were on our way to the doctor's home.

Dr. Derider was not due to open his office until nine that morning; therefore my father went directly to his house. It was seven when we got there. The goodly doctor had just finished preparing breakfast when the car screeched to a stop in his drive way. He took one look at my father's face and me hanging limply in his arms then, before daddy could speak he instructed us to drive to his office. We got there in five minutes; Dr. Derider pulled up two minutes later.

Between my father and Claudette, the doctor learnt I went to bed and, early in the morning, they found me in a state of unconsciousness with froth spewing from my mouth. No, I had not eaten or drank anything unusual, nor did I visit any strange place. Claudette started to tell them about her dream when my father stopped her. The doctor noticed but did not say a word. He reached for injection equipment and medicine and expertly pulled down my pants and injected the medicine in my buttocks. That's when I awoke with my father looking at me.

Claudette finished her story and looked at me. "Lester where is the sling shot?"

"Under di cellar," I answered, "but mi not throwing it 'weh."

"Yuh fadda say yuh must stop di bird shooting."

I sulked a bit but was shaken by the story and had decided I wasn't going to shoot any more birds. That weekend my Aunty Nerissa summoned me to her room. She was sitting on her bed looking directly at me.

"Yuh know yuh shoot Martha Cummings and it was her spirit dat lick yuh and nearly kill yuh?"

"Yes Aunty," I said meekly.

"Yuh have to be careful wid dat sling shot."

"Yes Ma'am."

"How yuh feel now son?"

"Ok Aunty."

"Neva mind, mi son. I fix dat wicked 'oman. She neva like yuh and deliberately come where yuh could shoot after her. Good spirit travel all around us but never trouble us. Dem nuh turn into bird and come where a boy with a sling shot will shoot dem. Ongle wicked, trouble making spirit do dat. All healthy boy pickney love fi ketch fish and shoot bird. Don't mek it stop yuh. She will never bodda yuh again."

When she was finished, Aunty Nerissa gave me a bosomy hug and told me to go have fun, as any good boy should.

I ran from her room as happy as can be. Needless to say, I have eaten lots of birds I personally shot several times since.

The storyteller ended his tale with a sadness and brusqueness uncharacteristic of him. But this atypical behavior began long before the story had ended. It started just about the middle when the old raconteur started glancing over his shoulder, pausing in mid sentence before continuing. Other times, he'd stare in the distance, over the heads of his listeners, as if distracted by something - an event unseen to us.

Many felt he was very tired while others thought he was just play-acting. But, like his fathers before him, he held his audience in utter enchantment despite the distractions. When the story ended, he bowed his now graying head, stared at his listeners and whispered, "Good night every one", then he was gone.

Mama was very disturbed. After making sure Dad was not ill, she returned and bade our friends and visitors farewell. The crowd scattered, many with questions on their lips. Before the night was over, rumour had it he was sick because a duppy boxed him. No one had seen a ghost except some troublemakers who claimed they saw a shadow on the steps beside daddy. This revelation stirred a great deal of concern with some of our close friends. They were anxious for my father's safety especially as it related to the future of his storytelling on Saturday nights.

I walked Dawn to her home and bade her goodnight. She was very concerned about my father and said that although she enjoyed the stories, she did not want to attend another session of storytelling.

I asked her why and her reply was simple, sounding just like mama. "I think the days of sitting outside and listening to stories are coming to an end. Though I enjoy it, I'd rather read a book or go to a movie."

"But I want to become a great storyteller," I protested.

"Then become one Cecil but tell it in books. Write your stories so many more people can enjoy them."

"Books?" I shouted incredulously.

"Yes, Cecil Jenkins - books." She turned into the walkway and slowly disappeared into her house.

When I got home, mama was still up. I had no idea what went wrong but mama comforted my sister and I, telling us daddy was tired and would be fine tomorrow. We went to bed, thrilled by a fine story, but sad at the turn of events.

After church the following Sunday, my mother told us what had happened. She said when they went to their room my father told her, "Isabel," he had said, "I will neva tell dat story again."

"Why Lesta? What happen?" she asked, but he shook his head negatively.

"In di mawnin' Isabel," he uttered wearily, "mi will tell yuh in di morning." Then he went to bed.

As soon as he awoke, mama asked him about last night's incident.

Daddy was quiet for a moment.

"Isabel, fi di secon' time I tell dis story something strange happen."

"What?"

"Di firs' time was in Jamaica, down by Jimmy..."

"Which Jimmy?"

"Yuh know Jimmy? Jimmy Pope dat have di bar dung di road from wi?"

"You mean drunkard Jimmy?"

"Well, yes."

"That ol' scoundrel!"

"Wha' wrong wid yuh? Mi t'ink yuh stop call people name."

"Ok, ok. Tell mi what happen'."

"Well, I was telling dem dis same story inna di bar wan day, when a had a strange feelin' a creep through mi body. Den mi head start fi swell and a could 'ardly breathe. Mi drop on de grung..."

"What?" interjected my mother, jumping from the bed, arms akimbo. "Lesta, you mean to tell me say, you faint inna bar an' never tell me anything all this time - eh?"

"Mek me finish nuh man."

"All right," she said, blowing hard in an outward show of anger.

"While mi lay dung pan di grung, mi vision di 'oman dem call Mana ... di same 'oman weh me jus' a talk 'bout. She come to me plain, plain. She a try fi tell me somet'ing but water full up hir eye and she couldn' talk. Den she turn an' walk weh."

"Lord have mercy," interrupted Mama, now very concerned.

Daddy continued: "Jimmy him get frighten, run fi di Bay Rum - rub me up and put it a mi nose. Di smell mus' a revive mi because' mi come to me self wid everyone roun' me."

"My God Lester, you could have died and nobody know 'bout it. I mean, yuh family would a know long after yuh dead. Gwaan man, finish yuh story."

"But Isabel, how come you a talk so much patois? Me t'ink yuh nuh like it at all."

Mama rolled her eyes and looked up at the ceiling, "Yuh know already, dat when mi ready, me can talk patois to."

"Yep! Mi know."

"Just tell me what happen man."

"After dat, Jimmy 'im fix some sweet sugar an water an give me fi drink. Mi feel a likkle betta but me head still feel a likkle funny. Den me figga seh is because me 'ungry, so me eat a piece a bun an' cheese an' drink di res' a sugar an' water. After dat, mi feel a likkle better. Me nuh tell dem nutten. Me jus' finish di story an' lef di bar."

My mother looked at him strangely, "How come yuh never tell me about this before?" she demanded.

"It wasn't nutten serious man. I was awright"

The bed creaked as she sat down sluggishly, leaning on both hands placed behind her like two poles holding up a mighty structure.

"So what happened last night?"

He shook his head slowly, over and over again, in inexplicable disbelief.

"Isabel," he said, "dis is what happen."

His story was frightening to say the least. Daddy told no one except my mother about the incident, and he never answered any questions about it except to say, "Wi have fi respec' di wishes of those gone by."

But mama spoke about it; he agreed she could and she did. The incredible episode began, that night, while he was in the middle of the story about 'The Duppy Bird'. He had gotten to the part where he said he grabbed his slingshot and crept close enough to get a good shot. He let the stone go and it hit the bird on the wing. It fluttered to the ground and he ran to pick it up. As he spoke, he saw a figure approaching him in the distance. Looking over the crowd, he tried to put a face to it, but couldn't. The person was heading straight for the group. It got closer and closer and finally sat on the ground in the back of everyone. But even after the figure sat, he couldn't make out a clear face. Every now and then the person, who he now realized was a black woman, waved her hand trying to tell him something, but he didn't understand and continued unperturbed.

According to Daddy, well into the story a cool breeze brushed his neck, he glanced around to see Mana standing by the door behind him. Not wanting to cause any disturbance, and realizing he was the only one seeing these figures, he continued telling the story as if nothing had happened.

Every now and again he looked back at Mana who never moved and stared unsmilingly at him. My father knew he was in the company of spirits, which were revealing themselves only to him. Though he knew Mana wanted to hurt him, the other spirit sitting on the ground seemed to be preventing her. He tried to behave normally, not wanting to arouse the curiosity of anyone in his audience. He was not aware that his constant looking around had already aroused the curiosity of many in his audience. After a while, it hit him like a bullet, jolting his very being. The apparition before him was his Aunty Nerissa and she was protecting him from Mana.

Aunty Nerissa seemed to smile as he relayed his story but the duppy behind him never smiled. Daddy did not feel fear but a deep sense of pre-eminence engulfed him, pushing him to continue telling the story, challenging him to do so without making anyone present aware of the spiritual presence in their midst. Then the spectre behind him spoke, whispering in his ears.

"Finish yuh story," the duppy said in a cold chilling voice only the storyteller could hear, "but when yuh done, don't ever talk 'bout mi again".

Daddy closed his eyes momentarily, when he opened it Mana was gone and his Aunty Nerissa began fading before his very eyes, vanishing as effortlessly as she had appeared, whispering eerily only for his ears: "Don't worry mi son she will never, never, never, never hurt you again."

Mama was dumbfounded when he finished speaking. No wonder he was acting so strange she thought. "Lester, you know people have all kinds of things to say?"

"Mek dem talk Isabel. Mek dem talk. It can't hurt me."

"But some people think yuh can't tell anymore stories."

"Ha, ha, ha, ha, ha hehehehehehe," Daddy laughed loudly. "Mi sure nah tell dat deh story again but me have nuff, nuff more story fi tell."

That week, he advertised his story for the next storytelling Saturday night. He said it was a true story about a boy and a grave next door to his house. It was to be one of the most frightening stories he had ever told.

Chapter 7

*a*pril rains brought cooler days, each evening the dying sun carried with it any remnant of daytime haze, ushering in unruffled moonlit nights of wondrous peace to our little town of Belle Glade. But there was no peace at the house of Lester Jenkins that Saturday night as people gathered with rising anticipation. Many, especially the children, voiced loads of unanswered questions: Did daddy actually see the two duppies two Saturdays ago? Did they seek to harm him? Will they allow him to tell his story today or will they appear again and maybe cause trouble? Will any harm come to them? The grownups were less afraid for their own safety but were still very concerned - especially for daddy. And yet his only response to all questions regarding the unpleasant episode was a single solitary sentence: "We have fi respect di wishes of those gone by." He simply refused to say anymore. This caused much curiosity amongst our visitors and they were even more intrigued about his stories.

Before daddy appeared that night, mother paraded through the crowd answering questions. She mollified them and suppressed their fears, altering their behavior and tranquilizing their moods of doom. Mama told them it was ok, that no one would get hurt, that the storyteller was healthy and strong, and would be telling stories for years to come. She convinced them that they were in no danger because, since the old days in Africa, the days of his fathers before him, no duppy had ever harmed any storyteller or his audience. Mother convinced the crowd that the power of good would always vanquish evil and my father, she knew, had the power of good on his side; he knew what he was doing.

Before she spoke to them, many had already voiced their opinions: some said the story was phony, it was contrived to create fear. But despite their noisy sentiments, no one disrespected daddy to his face. No, they never said an impolite word while he was present. And now that mama's bravura was over, once again they were like children awaiting the story-teller and his tale.

The place fell quiet when he appeared. Daddy surveyed the gathering much like a shepherd looks over his flock. He had heard all their speculations but none bothered him. To him, he had seen and heard what he had seen and heard and that's that. After all, the storyteller never lies.

"My friends," he said, "unno ready fi di story?"

A roar went up from the crowd. "Yes! Yes!" they shouted.

"Tonite, me ago tell unno 'bout a grave," daddy paused, "Di Grave Nex' Door," he shouted, hands held high.

The crowd roared as he took his regular seat on the top of the stairs. Daddy began.

The Grave Next Door

Long, long ago, the road leading from the village of Highgate, in St Mary, to the little town of Port Maria was not paved. It was nothing but a dirt track used by buggies, carts, and donkeys. No houses were built anywhere near the road. Just outside Highgate, on the way to Port Maria, is a little district called Harmony Hall. In those days, only three houses existed in the entire district of Harmony Hall and they were all located well away from the road, accessible only by a tiny dirt track leading from the road to the house.

An old lady named Liza Knight owned and lived in one of the houses. When she was born, her father planted her navel string in a small glass bottle with turpentine under a big Cotton Tree by the roadside. He believed something only few people ever heard about; if you put a baby's navel string in a glass of turpentine, closed it tightly, and plant it under a tree, it will not only ensure the baby's prosperity and strength but will protect the child from harm and evil throughout life.

It is said Liza owed her long life, perfect health, and riches to her father's belief and sagacity. He, however, died a relatively young age - only thirty-six years I believe.

When Liza was forty years old, the government, with the help of the landowners, began widening and paving the road. It was then she decided to cut down the large cotton tree even though it did not hinder the expansion of the road. The slave owner hated the big tree mostly because of the rumors concerning it. People, especially the slaves, were terribly afraid of the cotton tree, never traveling close to it after dusk. They chitchatted in quiet tones, telling tales of duppies living in the heart of the mighty tree. It had to go, Liza declared solemnly whenever conversations turned to the tree and now she had the perfect excuse so she leveled it with the help of outsiders. No man from the area, black or white, dared touch the gigantic trunk of the old cotton tree but Liza got the job done and, when it was over she was pleased, very pleased. The people of Harmony Hall awaited the trepidation, which never came - at least not then.

Liza did not know her ties to the enormously cotton. No! No one, not even her father, told her that her navel string was planted under the tree. She never even dreamed sixty-two years later, at the age of a hundred and two, she'd be buried on top of her own navel string at the same spot where the cotton tree once stood; such was dear Liza's fate.

Before she died, Liza made a will bequeathing her sixty-two acres of land to the twenty slaves she owned, along with enough money to purchase their freedom. Her only proviso was that any person getting the land with her grave on it, must keep it nicely weeded and clean. The rest of her money and jewelry was passed to her only daughter Casilda Knight, who left for England with no intentions of returning to Jamaica.

The plantation was divided in nineteen three-acre parcels and a five-acre lot where the remains of Liza Knight rested in the same spot where the big cotton had spread its branches providing shade with it thousands of little green leaves. Each of nineteen slaves received a three-acre parcel and the remaining slave, Timothy Salmon, inherited the five-acre piece with the grave.

By the time Alvin Salmon inherited the land, five generations of Salmons (Timothy, John, Alphy, Joe and Donald) had passed. Alvin's father, Donald Salmon, died in 1938 at the ripe old age of seventy-four, leaving him the land. Each generation of Salmon had respected Liza's wish and took good care of the grave.

Alphy Salmon, for example, in his days, paved the grave and placed a headstone on it. Only problem was he did not know the name of the person buried there, just that she was a white slave owner who had given the land to his great, great, great … grandfather. As a result, the headstone didn't carry a name but was crafted with the generic words:

Here Lies a Kind and Gentle Soul.
May She Rest in Eternal Peace.

The words were encased in neatly decorated artwork, very pleasing to the eyes.

Alvin, after inheriting the land and grave in 1938, built a house for his family close to the road about twelve yards from the grave. Two months later, the McPherson family from Annotto Bay, also bought a piece of the land and built a house adjacent to the grave on the other side of the Salmons, the grave abutting both houses.

Alvin's son, Caesar, was born June 1936, dead stamp of his father, short and pudgy with course black hair. Fat as he was, the boy enjoyed hectic games like kiting, fishing, and sprinting. But the runty lad also delighted in less propulsive games, like marbles and gigs, which were the fancy of the two McPherson boys. Hence, weekends and holidays found the trio playing all kinds of games on Liza's grave. Soon, their antics and boyish lack of regard for property left its mark on Liza's grave. The chipped grave-stone became a shadow of its former grandeur. Slashed, disfigured, and marked, its grimy surface matched the earth and grass surrounding it as cracks made intricate roadways on the broad cemented surface. Weeds grew randomly around its perimeter, trampled and flattened by six small feet that used it as their playground.

One day, in broad daylight, Caesar and his two friends, Benny and Keith McPherson, were playing, as usual, on Liza's grave. Caesar's mar-ble fell in a crevice between the concrete gravestone and the surrounding dirt. The boy searched in vain for his toy but the densely growing grass seemed to have hidden it. Then he saw the hole between the gravestone and dirt. His hand inched forward, index finger probing. It touched the grainy earth before disappearing in the hole. For a while, it hung suspended in midair, as if the hole had expanded into a small cavern. The boy twisted his finger, trying to feel the sides of the hole, desperately wanting to touch his marble. He forced it deeper then vigorously pulled it back as a dread-ful feeling, like an electric shock, shook his entire body. Screaming like a Banshee, he ran leaving behind his astonished friends staring and wonder-ing what had happened.

The seven-year-old boy dashed through the front door into his mother arms, weeping copiously, arms extended. Audrey Salmon heard her son's screams and ran towards him catching him in her arms.

"Hush, what wrong Caesar?"

"Mi han' mama, mi han'."

"What wrong wid yuh han'?"

"Me put it inna di grave mama."

"Which grave son?" she questioned, knowing the only possible grave he could have meant.

"Di grave nex' door."

"Come show mi son, come," she coaxed lifting him and walking out-side towards the grave next door. The two McPherson boys were still standing there, alarmed and baffled but not understanding what had happened to their friend. They both began gabbing at the same time.

"Caesar put 'im an' in a dat hole. Den wi jus' see 'im start bawl an' run to di 'ouse."

"Weh di hole?" asked Audrey, scrutinizing the spot where the boys were pointing.

"See it dere," exclaimed Benny pointing his finger at the exact spot.

Caesar pulled away from his mother's grasp, shrinking into the background, as she bent to study the hole. She placed her left hand in the opening, and then dragged it back. A sensation of weightlessness swelled her head and an unearthly smell oozed out of the hole. She pulled herself to her feet and staggered back.

"Keith an' Benny? Go to yuh madda. NOW!" she shouted. The boys ran towards their house as she pulled her son by the hand stumbling towards their house. Once inside the protection of her dwellings, the feelings passed. Audrey sat hugging her son for a long while, neither person speaking. What caused the terrible smell and why did she feel woozy? These were the questions twirling in her head as she stared in space rocking backwards and forward.

The answers came to her in a rush: somehow the grave was opened and the coffin, now rotten, caused the decayed flesh to smell and seeped through the hole. The dreadful smell must have caused her head to swell. But what had hurt Caesar's hand? She pondered. Maybe an ant or some other insect bit the poor baby. Satisfied she propped herself up carefully easing her son into the seat.

"Want somet'ing fi drink Caesar?"

"Yes mama."

She poured a mug of sugar and water, cooled by a piece of ice left over from the penny ice she bought earlier that morning. Caesar drank thirstily and was soon his old self, huffing and puffing because his mother wouldn't allow him outside for the rest of the day.

Later, when Alvin got home from his field Audrey told him what had happened.

"But dat grave deh is a ol', ol' grave yuh nuh Audrey. Anyone bury deh, mus' be rotten an' gone, long, long time. Yuh couldn' smell nutten even if the grave did open up."

"Den what mi smell an' why mi feel giddy?"

"Ah feel seh is a duppy trouble unno."

"Duppy?" responded Audrey in amazement.

"Yes!"

"In broad daylight?"

Alvin thought about it for a while then a slow whistle escaped his lips. "Kiss mi neck! A di 'oman weh bury deh yuh nuh."

Audrey shrunk back in astonishment, her eyes wide, her face furrowed, and her breathing heavy. "Di white 'oman weh yuh fadda tell we 'bout?" she squeaked.

"Eh, heh," he said, shaking his head sending undulations rippling through his fat neck. Audrey looked at her husband; the white of his eyes always surprised her, contrasting sharply with the black pupil and smooth black skin covering his pudgy round face. Now the pearly white eyes rolled in his head betraying the fear he felt.

"Audrey, we not been taking care a di grave like me granpappy seh."

"Yes Alvin. Yuh really t'ink a di 'oman vex because we nuh clean di grave?"

"Eh, heh."

"Den mek wi go clean it tomorrow nuh?"

"Nuh mus' man. Firs' t'ing in di mawnin'."

And he was as good as his words. Early the following morning, Alvin gathered his cutlass, file and pickaxe. He spent much of the day clearing the grave and the area around it. He mixed cement and filled in the cracks after thoroughly washing the headstone. The job was finished by 1:30 p.m. Alvin called Audrey and they both surveyed the grave. Satisfied they walked away; the job was well done and the grave looked brand new.

At about five a.m. one Friday morning, not long after the grave was cleaned, Babba, a young man of eighteen from Harmony Hall, walked from his house to meet his girlfriend living on Gully Road just outside the town of Highgate. The couple planned to spend the morning together at her house, and then travel by the early bus to Port Maria. As he sauntered up the dark Harmony Hall road, his thoughts were far away. He was thinking about beautiful Pagge Beach, its mile of firm soft sand and crystal clean, clear, warm water. The young man was so intently focused on his daydream that he was unafraid of the darkness. He smiled as he envisioned himself relaxed, his girl beside him, on rustic Pagge beach. He saw fishing boats, people walking along the beach, kids playing, and a brilliant sunshine. His steps were soft and sure as he marched towards his destination.

Babba jerked to reality when he saw a lady standing at the side of the road. She stood between the McPherson and Salmon houses, adjacent to the old grave that Alvin Salmon cleaned last week. He approached warily, finding it odd that a female would be standing alone at the side of the road at this time of the morning. As he advanced, she stepped to the middle of the road. A sickening feeling washed over him and he stopped and peered at her.

The lad couldn't discern a face but it was clear the person was a white woman. What the hell was a white woman, dressed in a full white gown flowing to her ankle, doing in Harmony Hall, in the middle of the road, at this time of the morning? He wondered. Strange as it seemed and terrible as he felt, he simply had to go about his business. He stepped to his right in an attempt to go around her but the woman moved to her left blocking his advance. He stepped back and moved quickly to his left she was faster and blocked his advance again. He stubbornly slipped to his right again knowing it was a vain attempt to bypass her. To his astonishment, the woman began to grow, spreading her white dress until it covered the full width of the road. It was then that he knew, for sure, he was dealing with a duppy.

In one sudden movement, Babba spun and dashed down the road screaming dreadfully - on top of his voice.

"Lawd Jeesas, 'elp me…Whoooooooooey, Lawd have mercy. Help!"

The poor lad ran as fast as his feet could take him, and didn't stop until he hit the front door leading to his father's house, crashing hard against the structure, shoulder first. The door crashed inwards under his powerful weight, awakening the entire house. He burst into the house crying continuously, "Is a duppy, a 'oman duppy. Help! No mek she ketch me. Help ooh, help!"

It took more than ten minutes for his father and mother to calm the lad who, wild eyed, didn't want to say a word except that he saw a 'duppy woman'. The household sat in vigil for the rest of morning but no duppy entered the house.

Babba was unable to talk for three days. His parents took him to Dr. Henry in Highgate who found nothing wrong and said he couldn't help him at all. For two straight days after the doctor's visit, the young man only ate small pieces of bread and drank water. Then on the third day, Mr. Taylor, his father, decided to take him to see 'Bredda' Toby Dixon, the Pocomania preacher and local obeah man.

"Bredda Toby," he said holding on to Babba's hand, "one duppy lick mi boy and him cyaan eat or talk."

"Mi know," responded the obeah man, shaking his head in unsurprised acknowledgement.

Mr. Taylor did not seem stunned at the guzzu man's response and continued: "Mi want yuh fi 'elp di bwoy."

"Eh, eh, yuh come a di right place." Then he beckoned to the man, "Come ya. Come ya fi a minute." They stepped aside from the boy. "It gwine cos' yuh five pound, yuh nuh?"

"A nuff money dat" he paused as if pondering the cost. "Is alright," he said shaking his head in acknowledgement.

"Lef' half a it now an' when yuh come back yuh carry di res'."

Mr. Taylor pulled out two pounds and ten shillings from his hip pocket and handed it to the obeah man.

"Lef' yuh son wid me and come back lata' fi im."

" 'Bout one a clock?"

"Eh, heh. Good time. 'Im wi' alright. Nuh worry."

The Poco preacher took Babba's hand and led him towards his dwelling while Mr. Taylor left for home.

No one except 'Bredda' Toby, not even Babba, knew what happened next. The obeah man asked the boy to sit on a stool in a strange room smelling strongly of essence, with candles, bibles, bones, and flags strewn all over the room. Opposite the stool, a red and blue cloth lined with yellow sash covered a narrow but high dais and a long cross - almost touching the ceiling - extended from its right side. On the other side of the dais, a polished wooden staff rested idly as if awaiting some sinister use. The staff, about ten feet long, had the head of a ram goat expertly engraved on the upper end. The rest of its length rippled with the carving of a curling snake wrapped around its length, its tail forming the tip of the staff.

The obeah man lit three candles and offered the boy a glass of yellowish liquid, motioning him to drink. The boy downed the liquid while the man chanted a few words in a strange language, picking up and wielding the staff in a foreign dance. As he approached, the boy felt inebriated, both man and staff appeared shadowy, then he knew no more. When he awoke, his father had returned and he was lying exhausted on a bench on the obeah man's veranda. The boy looked around puzzled, what was he doing here?

How did he get here? he wondered, opening his eyes wide, standing and stretching; gradually his head cleared and he began to focus. Then he remembered, ah yes, the obeah man gave him something to drink then everything went blank. The adrenalin started to flow and he began to feel great. Babba saw his father and Bredda Toby at the same time, and asked for a drink of water, which he drank thirstily. The water dropped like lead in his empty stomach.

"Papa," he said, "mi hungry."

Mr. Thomas looked at his son realizing he had fully recovered. His words were clear and he seemed steady and alert. "Yuh wi'get food when wi reach home Babba," the man promised.

Mr. Taylor was happy, he paid preacher Dixon the balance and walked away with his son. After eating a full plate of food, Babba told his father his story of the encounter with the duppy woman for the first time. Both father and son knew who the duppy was and the young man decided never to walk alone at nights past the grave again, but it was to be the beginning of many strange incidents at the site of the grave next door.

Over the next two years, only small incidents occurred in the area surrounding the grave next door. People reported smelling strange and disgusting scents, unrecognized sounds, uncommon puffs of wind and the now and then fleeting but distinct sightings of a shadowy white woman. The area became well known as a duppy spot and local residents grew very cautious when traveling at nights within the vicinity.

The McPhersons sold their place and moved to Kingston shortly after Babba confronted the apparition. A man named John Cooley bought it. He, his eleven-year-old son Barry, and ten-year-old daughter Moffett moved into the house a few months later. The Cooley's had relatives - John's younger brother Frank and his older sister Nicey - living up the road a few chains past the deep bend in the road they called Steel Curve.

Frank Cooley was only fourteen in the summer of '38, the year he moved to Harmony Hall, and so he was playmate to his cousins Barry and Moffett. John Cooley was a 'higgler' who traveled to Spanish Town market every Thursday morning to sell his bananas ripened with carbine (local name for Calcium Carbide). He stayed in Spanish Town all day Thursday, Friday and Saturday, returning Saturday night. On these days, John employed Mable Wilson, a local helper, to stay with and care for his children.

Most Friday nights, Frank joined his cousins Barry and Moffett at their house to play games, normally cards, but when the game was over he was afraid to travel home alone. He was mortified at the very thought of walking alone around the dark bend called Steel Curve. Barry and Moffett enjoyed his company; he was a good card player and provided added company and exciting competition. To bribe Frank, the brother and sister promised to accompany him as far as the edge of Steel Curve where lamplight shone brightly, from windows of surrounding houses, lighting up the area. The pair was very scared themselves and did not want to pass Steel Curve. Frank agreed, as long as they would stay and watch while he ran through the darkness and enter his house before they leave. And so, it became a matter of habit for Barry and Moffett to accompany Frank to the edge of Steel Curve on Friday nights.

It was a dark night on Friday August 5, 1938; the moon was nowhere in sight when Barry and Moffett Cooley followed Frank to the edge of Steel Curve, eleven thirty that night. They watched Frank run to his house before the brother and sister set out trotting on their way back home. In the distance, they saw a lady ambling along in the general direction they were heading. Happy for company they increased their speed in an effort to catch up. Suddenly, they realized the faster they ran the further away the lady appeared, even though she seemed to be walking very slowly. Fear seized the kids but they had to reach home.

Panic ensued as they realized the lady had stopped just short of their house beside the grave. They had heard many stories about the grave next door and the lady who was buried there. But they had to get home; they must pass the lady even though she stood frighteningly close to their gate as if daring them to pass. The boy on the inside close to the lady, the girl abreast of him they dashed down the road in an attempt to breeze pass the duppy. Their young hearts in their mouths, they hoped to zip pass her and make a desperate dash into their house.

As they came abreast of the duppy, Barry began skidding in one spot while his sister dashed through the gate on her way into the house. The boy felt powerful hands holding him by the back of his pants waist, hoisting him off the ground, his foot moving as if still running but with no forward movement; his sister now gone into their house. It was then he remembered the popular claim that duppies hated curse words (called 'bad words' in Jamaica). Without thinking further the boy began cursing.

"Let me go yuh &%$#@ rotten belly 'oman," the boy cried, kicking and cursing loudly. Suddenly, he fell forward, both feet hitting the ground as the duppy released him. Barry stumbled and nearly fell but quickly gained his foot and sped for the front door of his house where Mable and Moffett anxiously waited him. Crying and blowing heavily, the lad rushed inside and Mable quickly closed the door behind them.

Barry couldn't speak immediately, so tired and frightened he was but Mable held him and gently lead him to a chair. Moffett cuddled her brother crying quietly tears running down her pretty little face. After a few minutes, the helper ushered the two kids into the main bedroom. Where all three of them huddled into one bed – John Cooley's bed that night. No one wanted to be alone.

The following day, Alvin and Audrey Salmon visited their neighbours to inquire why was young Barry cursing and at the top of his voice late last night. They told the trio they were very surprised at the boy's behavior and had every intention of reporting the incident to his father on his return. The two children and Mable sat and relayed the whole incident to the couple.

"So di duppy 'oman still a trouble people eh?" said Alvin.

"What we mus' do fi stop it?" his wife asked, obviously very disturbed.

"Mi nuh know but mi haffi do somet'ing."

"Mi nah go out a door once night come" said Barry.

"Me to," his sister said, shaking her head negatively, the furrows on her face clearly revealing her fears.

The Salmons, realizing the desperation of the situation, not knowing when this duppy woman may actually hurt one of these children or some other poor soul, knew something must be done. They left their neighbour's house very disturbed. They couldn't understand it. The grave looked immaculate; it had been cleared and cleaned. They had made certain to keep it clean and no one played on it or in the immediate area anymore. They had forbidden their son to even go near the place. Why, they wondered, why hadn't the spirit of the woman buried there gone to rest? Why was she still haunting the neighbourhood? Something had to be done about it and soon. The Salmons had no idea what to do except visit the local obeah man and they were not ready to do so yet. The days past without incident causing the Salmons to forget the duppy woman until the duppy appeared again harming someone very innocent.

Bredda Toby married sister Kissy, a waspish, loudmouth and quarrelsome woman from the neighbourhood. Since hitching up with the goodly preacher, she made certain the local women were afraid to even look at the obeah man, or so she thought. Before they were married, he had eleven children with ten different women. Only Sissy, who died seven years ago, had two children for him.

Each and every one of his children's mothers was a member of his church congregation, his flock. Most Sundays, they all swarmed to the little whitewashed building they called church because they knew he wanted them there. Though the pastor was known to support all his children, he was very generous to those who obeyed his bidding and attended service. After all, some of the same money he gave them for child support came back as collection, which he gave to them again. Moreover, they loved the Pocomania way of life. It was the only way they knew how to serve the true and living God.

Sister Kissy had a boy before the marriage and a girl after marrying the preacher. In all, Bredda Toby had twelve children alive; one had died six months after birth.

What no one, especially Sister Kissy, knew was that Rachael Moore, from Islington, had a little boy, three years old, for Bredda Toby. Rachael was only sixteen years old when she became pregnant. Her angry mother wanted to expose the 'wutless dutty parson' in her words, but because Bredda Toby was so glib and free of hand with his money, he won her over and she did nothing about it.

True to his words, the preacher gave a generous amount of money to Ms. Moore and her daughter, for the child each and every month, without fail. He loved this child, whom he named Richard, more than any of his other children because little Richard's skin was fair. His mother had long 'pretty' black hair, small straight nose, thin lips, and almost looked white with 'nice blue' eyes. The baby boy looked just like his mother, handsome and fair, could pass for a little white baby boy.

One Friday evening, Rachael came to Highgate to collect money for her child. The boy was now three years of age and once or sometimes twice per month, she made this trek and oftentimes stayed by her cousin in Cromwell Land until Saturday morning she'd take the bus home. Oftentimes, the preacher met her at her cousin, stayed with her for part of the night and then returned home. They were never seen together on the streets of Highgate town or Harmony Hall. Sometimes, she met him secretly at a shop close to his home in Harmony Hall, and then she'd walk to Cromwell Land to her cousin. They were always exceptionally careful when they met close to his house. After all, Sister Kissy would kill them both if she ever found out. There were the times when he'd visit her in Islington but she preferred the trips to Highgate as she enjoyed the bus ride and getting away from her home.

On this Friday night, Bredda Toby did not show up at her cousin's house as planned. She was baffled because he had specifically asked her to take little Richard with her. He had not seen the child for over a month and longed to see him. Rachael wondered if she had made a mistake in thinking he wanted them to meet at her cousin, rather than at the shop near to him. At around five thirty that evening, although she knew it was getting late, she decided to walk to the shop in Harmony Hall where she was sure he'd be waiting. Rachael and her son arrived at the shop about six thirty that evening but the preacher was not there. After spending an hour and a half chitchatting with the shopkeeper, the obeah man still had not turned up. At eight o'clock, Rachael decided to walk back to Cromwell Land with her baby boy.

The moon was out and a few people were still walking along the road so Rachael was not afraid. She did hear stories about the duppy woman who haunted the area surrounding the Salmon house and knew they had to pass the very spot to reach her destination but the young girl anticipated no trouble. She held little Richard in her arms, his head resting on her shoulder, a thumb in his mouth sucking contentedly. The duo moved hurriedly past the Salmons' without incident. She just got comfortable believing the worse was past when little Richard began to cry and shake. She hugged him loosely, scrutinizing his features, trying to determine what was wrong. Suddenly the child went limp, his eyes rolled and he began to froth at the mouth. Frightened now, she ran towards the first house with rays of light streaming through a window. Knocking frantically on the door she began to cry for help.

"Help! Help! Help!" she shouted, desperately watching her son's eyes spinning grotesquely, froth pumping from his mouth.

"Is who dat?" came a woman's voice.

"Mi son a dead Ma'am, help, help, please."

The door swung back swiftly and a middle-aged woman took one look and pulled her into the house, little Richard cradled in her arms.

"What happen? Put 'im pan di bed. Lawd Jeesas. Morris," she

wheezed, blowing as if she had just lifted a thousand pounds, "Morris! Morris" she shouted, "come 'ear now. Right now!"

The side door opened and an old man walked in. "What's di matter Martha?"

"Duppy mus' a lick dis poor pickney. Bring di bible an' rub up sum Ramgoat Roses, Piaba, an' Guinea Grass in di kitchen. Put likkle water an' olive ile in deh, an' bring it come. An' Morris, mix likkle a di Chainy Root wid di cod liva ile fi 'im drink. Before she was finished, the old man was gone. In the twinkling of an eye, he was back with an old bible and disappeared again. Rachael undressed her son while Martha stomped the floor reading aloud from Psalm 91.

"He who dwells in the shelter of the Most High will rest in the shadow of the almighty... Lawd help dis chile." Her bare feet slapped the floor loudly. The old man appeared with a mug and saucer in hand.

"Rub im up Morris an' gi im di liquid fi drink. Lawd 'elp wi." While Rachael poured the liquid down the child's throat, Morris rubbed the mixture on his chest and Martha held the bible to the light.

"... You will not fear the terror of night, nor the arrow that flies by day, nor the pestilence that stalks in the darkness, nor the plague that destroys at midday... Lawd have mercy on us all!"

With every verse she read, she stomped the floor. Soon little Richard stopped frothing, his eyes relaxed and he fell asleep, his mother rocking him from her lap. Martha did not stop reading the bible until the entire chapter was finished. Then she turned to Rachael and said, "Unno can't leave here tonight. Stay till a mawnin'."

"Yes Ma'am," the girl answered meekly.

Then the old man Morris looked at her quizzically, "But yuh nuh Miss Moore from Islington daughta?" the old man observed.

"Yes sah."

"A fi yuh chile dis?"

"Yes sah."

"A who a 'im pupa?"

Rachael fell silent wanting to keep this information as guarded as possible. The old man had heard the rumors but paid them no attention before now.

"Ahoe," he bowed his head over and over, in stark realization, "a Bredda Toby a di fadda nuh?"

The girl shot him a frightful glance, but the old man continued. "Nuh mind me dear, wi always mind wi own business. Wi nuh have nutten fi seh to anybody."

The old man looked away and behaved as if he had never asked a question. That night, the boy and his mother slept at Martha and Morris Peynado's house. Early in the morning they walked to their cousin's house in Cromwell Land, just in time to relieve a very worried cousin who was about to travel all the way to Islington to ensure that every thing was ok with Rachael and her son. Throughout the early morning, little Richard slept then at mid morning he awoke crying, holding and moving his head as if he was having a throbbing headache. Rachael realized the bush medicine and prayers had worked wonderfully for him in healing his ailment from whatever the duppy did to him. She divided a tablet in two and gave half to the child. Then she fed him and put him to bed again. When he awoke in the afternoon, the boy was still woozy but the crying had stopped. That evening, they both boarded the bus for Islington.

Little Richard Dixon did not recover completely for over two weeks. He developed a fever as soon the hot days were over and the cool nights rolled in. During these evening times, Rachael and her mother rubbed him with bush medicine and Bay Rum, which seem to help a little. Bredda Toby still had no idea of what had happened to his favourite son. Then one day, the boy's grandmother visited his father in Harmony Hall and told him what had happened. Bredda Toby nearly went out of his mind. Demons couldn't hold him back from visiting his son.

The preacher said he was so caught up with a client he had forgotten everything about their planned meeting that Friday evening. He hugged his son and promised never to ever let anything like this happen to him again. Bredda Toby asked Rachael and her mother to leave him alone with the boy for a few minutes. When they were alone the Pocomania man worked a little guzzu to ensure the boy's continuing health. He opened the door to let the family in, a sanguine grin of satisfaction on his face. That day, the obeah man left for home, with one thing on his mind, to deal with the duppy woman once and for all.

The night was jet black when the Poco preacher presented himself at the grave of Liza Knight. He stood alone, a staff in his left hand and a long guava branch in his right. The air was still while the moon obediently floated across the skies, casting shadows on the ground. When the clock struck twelve, the plucky obeah man struck the grave with the guava branch chanting, "Calusa umbra come forth, Calusa umbra come forth." Three times he clobbered the grave and three times he chanted. On the third chant, the night stood still, not an insect stirred, he held the staff in the air like the sword of Genghis Khan, shielding himself from the grave. She appeared at the headstone as if by magic. The spectre danced and approached as he held the staff before him preventing her from getting too close. The man spoke fast and sharp. "What yuh doing ere? Why yuh not gone to res'?"

The duppy woman moved closer, shying away from the staff, then she whispered, "Can't rest."

"Why? Yuh grave clean. Dem tek good care a it."

"Not the grave. It's my navel string."

"What 'bout yuh navel string?"

"The coffin rests on it."

"What?"

"They buried me on my navel string."

"Ahoe," he said bowing his head in acknowledgement, "me understan'."

Duppy and man stood still for a moment then he said, "Why yuh trouble mi boy?"

"I didn't mean any harm, just playing. Only playing." Her voice faded and she was gone.

The obeah man sat on the grave pondering his encounter for a long time. Then he knew what he'd do. The following day he visited Alvin Salmon.

"Mr. Salmon," he began, "we have to dig up di coffin weh into di grave next door."

"Dig up di coffin? Man yuh mad."

"No sah," he said shaking his head. "If yuh want di duppy weh live roun yah fi leave, we have fi dig it up."

"What? How it we 'elp?"

"Dem bury di 'oman pon her navel string. A t'ink dem put hir navel string inna turpentine and bury hit dear, then when she dead dem dig di grave same place. Di navel string must be plant deep, deeper dan the grave. So when dem dig di grave dem still neva reach di navel string and put di coffin ova di navel string. Now di duppy cyaan dig up di sinting an' she can't rest till hit dig up an' bury proppa."

"My God man, how yuh know?"

"No worry 'bout dat, jus' mek wi dig it up."

Alvin Salmon never really liked Bredda Toby but the obeah man had a reputation as being very good with duppies in the district. Alvin had to believe him and was ready to try anything to get rid of the duppy living in the grave next door.

The next day, the two men met and with the help of four others, from the district, dug up the rotten coffin from the grave next door. As they dug under the grave they found it, a bottle in good condition, sunk deep in the earth. After washing the bottle they saw that the original liquid inside had dried up leaving only a rusty dirty spot. Bredda Toby Morris would not allow anyone to open the bottle, ordering the men to place it in the rotten coffin and rebury everything as it was before.

Alvin remade a tomb with a beautiful headstone, with money collected from a few caring parishioners. Two weeks later, the Pocomania preacher told his congregation that the spirit was at rest. "Yes," he said, "she was gone forever."

No one doubted him and no one ever saw a duppy in the area again. Not even to this day.

Daddy finished his story a tired man. It was fairly dark because mama had turned off the veranda lights just before he started his story, leaving only one light at the side of the house. Not only did the night seem cooler but daddy's storytelling took on new dimensions, evoking an eerie feeling all around. The children were afraid and some grown ups were also terrified. Most people did not want to walk home alone and many would be sleeping uncomfortably that night but they all enjoyed the story.

As the group dispersed, people talked about Jamaica and the reality of duppies. They reflected on ghost sightings in their own area. The children played jokes on each other while the grown ups impressed one another by courageously pretending, for the benefit of the children, that they were unafraid.

Mother told me what happened later that same night. Daddy had asked her if she enjoyed the story.

"I did Lester," she responded, "you are a truly great storyteller."

Daddy sat on the bed his chin in his hand. He looked at mother with new respect. She had tolerated him all these years, allowed him his greatest pleasure without ever interfering or questioning his actions. Oh how strange life is, he thought. Had it not been for the children he might not have returned to Jamaica during the winter of '49. But the miserable, bossy woman had grown to become an angel and his only true friend. He reflected on the past years and realized she had been miserable because she wanted the best for her family. He was not working in Jamaica and her family was getting nothing and were beginning to suffer. Today, they were not hungry; they had a good business and a little money in the bank. He had visited Jamaica a few times over the years and wished his son had gotten to know the place better. He had one desire before he passed from this life and that was to visit Africa, where his forefathers once lived. Daddy looked at mama long and hard.

"Isabel, I have held back a few stories that I have been saving for my son. I want him to know them so he will have fresh new stories to tell when the time is right."

She gaped at him eyes wide open. "Lester you just spoke to me in perfect English?"

"Yes," he said simply.

"But Lester all these years the only time you speak properly is when you are telling your stories. Look how me cuss you and quarrel. You never change, but now you decide to do it. Why Lester, why?" She was not quarrelling, she was not reprimanding him, she simply could not understand.

Lester Jenkins sighed, "My dear Isabel, I believe patois is the African man's language. Like my storytelling, it is just one of the few things we have for ourselves. We should not destroy it and we should never let anyone take it from us. We have been foolish, calling our own language negrish and bad. It is the language our forefathers before us created so they could understand each other, the language they made with their own tongues and minds. We should be proud of it. I did not mean to be insulting to you my dear when I used it every chance I got, but I knew you wouldn't understand. Today, we have grown to love and respect each other and I know you do understand. Am I right?"

"Yes Lester," she said wonderingly.

"Anyway my wife, my son is a good storyteller but I am afraid he doesn't have enough storytelling material, especially out of Jamaica. He may have heard many American ghost stories but still I don't know if he has enough stories to tell. The boy has got to gather new material. I want him to begin telling his own stories. It is time he takes over storytelling

Saturday nights."

Mama sighed loudly. After all these years, she thought, her husband still hadn't truly seen the changing wind of time. She decided to give
it one more try.

"Les, in these new days storytelling is changing. More people are
going to the movies and television is taking over. Our son will need all the
material he can get from you, but he will not be able to carry on the tradition for long, even if we all wanted it. We must realize what is happening
and be prepared for the changes. Cecil has to prepare himself for life in his
days. Storytelling days are your days and storytelling, as we know it, is
dying. Don't you see it Les? It is dying."

Daddy was quiet for a long moment. Then soberly he said, "Dying
Isabel but not dead. There is still time for our son."

"No! No, no Lester. It's too late for our son."

"Then what should he do Isabel? All his life he has wanted nothing
else. What can we tell him to do?"

Daddy was losing his conviction and mama saw it. He was defeated
and she sensed victory but it was not the sweet victory she yearned for. It
was the bitter, hollow feeling one gets from watching a loved one perish -
shrivel and die. "The same thing I've been always telling him to do for the
past five or more years Les," she forced herself to say.

"Well tell me again Isabel," he muttered, "tell me what we should have
our boy do with his life."

She didn't believe he really wanted her to say it so she continued, "He
should have done it long ago Lester. Long, long ago."

"You still haven't told me what we should do, you know."

"He should have studied harder. He shouldn't have spent his time
engrossed in duppy stories. Now it's time for college and we don't know
which college will accept him or what he is going there to do. The boy is
not prepared."

"You want the boy to come out an' go work for one of them white people Isabel? Don't you see it's no different from working the cane fields? It's
only that the work may not be so hard and dirty and the pay maybe, just
maybe, a little more."

"No Lester, he could learn a profession and come out and work for himself."

The last words were hardly out of mama's mouth when the thought hit
him. He saw it clearly. Yes, yes, his son would definitely become a story-

teller - if he really wanted to.

"My God Isabel, you're right", he shouted with renewed strength. The boy can become a writer. Take the stories and sell them," he paused, reality cutting away at his wonderful idea. Then he whispered more to himself than to his wife, "If he knew how."

Mama smiled, shaking her head in satisfaction. Now he truly realized and understood what she was saying. "But is it too late Isabel? I mean - is it too late for the boy to learn? Can't he learn writing in college?"

"Yes my husband," she said cheerfully, standing and walking towards the bathroom, "but it depends on how well he does in his exams the end of this semester." Her words lingered in the room as she departed closing the bathroom door behind her.

Daddy mulled the idea pacing the floor until mama reappeared.

"How is he doing so far?" It was the first time he ever inquired about my school work in all his life.

"Average."

"Then we must talk to him," he said excitedly. "Tomorrow, first thing we will talk to him Isabel. One more thing, I want the boy to go to Jamaica for a short while. Just to learn how it is there today, to get new and good material and visit the graves of his own people. What do you say?"

"It's a good idea my husband."

"He can stay with his uncle Roger in Highgate."

"Eh, heh."

"How about us Isabel?"

"What do you mean, Lester?"

"What do you want, my dear?"

"Nothing. I have all I want."

"Well then let us both go to Africa for a while. Let us take a vacation."

Before he knew it, she was hugging him and kissing him. I am so happy Lester. It's exactly what I always wanted to do."

"Me too my dear, me too."

"But what about Pamela, what will we do with her? She will feel so left out."

"Remember her holidays are coming up soon. We will take her with us or if she want, she can stay with Carmen."

"Yes, of course you are right. We'll ask her. Give her the choice."

My mother and father went to bed very content that night. The next day my father called us all together. We sat around the table, all four of us. He told us, to our delight, of the plans they had made the night before. Then daddy surprised me with his next words.

"Son," he said, "I want you to listen to me carefully. All your life you wanted to become a storyteller, true?" I shook my head in agreement.

"Well Cecil it can't happen like we planned." Everyone around the table saw the astonish glare in my eyes. They saw the anguish, the misery pulling taunt every muscle in my body forcing me to stand.

"What? What do you mean daddy?" I managed, moving away from the table as if afraid of the answer.

"Sit son. Just listen to what I have to say." Mama stretched her hand as if to steady my approach but it was the hands of sympathy and love though I didn't know it then. My sister sat passively watching me, her hands in her lap, her eyes the essence of sadness and compassion.

I sat lamely, half perched on the edge of my chair, leaning towards daddy, one hand on the table the other resting lifelessly in my lap.

"Your mother has been right all along son. The days of storytelling is dying. You will not have the audience I have had. Only the old folks are interested in storytelling these days."

"That's not true daddy," I shot back interrupting him.

"Think about it Cecil. How many of the younger ones come here these days? Only your good friends. And many times they don't come because they are gone to the movies. What about the younger ones? Do they come to listen to me? Not anymore son."

True as it was, I wanted to hear no more. "I'm going to become a good storyteller daddy and nothing can stop me. I'll be better than you daddy. You just watch and see." I averted my head in a vain attempt to hide the tears welling up in my eyes.

"I know son. I know how you feel."

"Listen to me Cecil," my mother interjected a little sternly. "I know you are a good storyteller already. But you must move with the times. You must realize it is no longer the time to sit outside in the night air and tell duppy stories. No one is going to continue to support that sort of thing.

But you can still tell your stories, to a lot more people than will visit our house and you can make a living doing it."

I wasn't listening to Mama. I didn't want to hear her. All I knew was I was definitely going to sit on that upper step and tell my stories. People would cheer, or laugh, or cry but they would love my stories and keep coming back for more. I was sure I could do it and the younger folks would enjoy it also.

"Mama? Mama? MAMA?" my screaming voice filled the small room with the boom of a cannon. She stopped talking abruptly and all three stared intently at me. "I am a storyteller," I snarled, dashing to my room.

They left me alone then but I knew they would be back; later, tomorrow, or the next day, they would be back and it wouldn't be long.

And it was only a day later before they cornered me again. "Son?" Daddy said shaking his head in his usual manner and reverting to his usual patois, "yuh have to listen to wi. Yuh madda say, if you become a good writer you could make a whole heap of money and wi would be proud a yuh."

"But daddy, how can I become a good writer and write books? Only white people write books - or rich black people! People like us tell stories, they don't write books."

Mama stepped in then, "Rubbish," she said, "all you need is the ability to tell interesting stories and know English good enough to put it on paper. But you have to study English. Go to college and get a degree. Son, we will support you as long as you go to college. No matter which college as long as you can study English."

"You mean I can write the same stories daddy have been telling and turn it into a book?"

"Yes," they said together. I was mighty confused, where were my dreams going? How could they stand there and destroy all my dreams like this?

"But can I still tell stories as long as people want to hear them?"

"Yes my son, you can," daddy said but mother stared at me soberly and shook her head negatively.

"Who will you tell when you have gone away to college son? Eh? Who?"

"I can go to a college close by."

"We were thinking of New York."

I remembered Dawn then and quelled my objection until I knew more about her plans. Truthfully, the idea of writing a book never occurred to me before, even though Dawn had suggested it a couple of nights before. Dawn! Dawn! Her name kept popping into my head whenever a decision had to be made.

Suddenly, I felt weak. What was I thinking? Daddy had a storytelling night coming up in two weeks time and everyone was talking about it. Surely they were wrong. Why would so many people be excited about daddy's storytelling and yet say it was dying? If I graduate from high school next term, I can get a job in one of the businesses downtown as an accounting clerk just like Hopi Kaneohe, my Indian friend who graduated last year. He was making good money and we studied the same subjects. Hopi said it wasn't hard work and he worked only Mondays through Fridays from eight in the morning to five in the evenings. That would leave me all day Saturday to prepare my story for Saturday night.

It was clear to me that my plans as a storyteller would work very well. There seem to be no other way. Yes! My mother and father were wrong. I was sure. I'll show them, I thought, I'll show them.

Chapter 8
Dawn

*D*awn was waiting for me at the little shop downtown where we often met. I told her about my parents' plans to go to Africa and the wonderful vacation I was going to have in Jamaica but I didn't mention anything about college.

"Cecil man," she said playfully, her slant Chinese eyes seemed almost shut, "tell them to buy two tickets nuh."

"Would you come with me for two whole weeks in Jamaica?" I queried.

"Of course," she laughed, holding my hands and spinning me around mischievously. I looked at her and my breath stuck in my throat, as my heart hammered. She had that effect on me every time she smiled, flashing pearly white teeth that glistened in the sun; her long shaggy jet-black hair twirling around her sleek little neck like a lion's mane.

"Seriously Dawn, suppose we can find the money to pay your fair?"

The playfulness disappeared and she answered in a serious tone. "Come on Cecil, no. You know my parents wouldn't allow me and why would I go to Jamaica with you alone? You're crazy."

"Why not?"

"Because it's not proper."

"What's not proper? I am seventeen and you are sixteen. We are almost grown ups."

"Almost Cecil. That's only almost. We are not adults. And even if we were, it would still be wrong."

"Why?" I insisted.

She tilted her head and rolled her eyes in that 'are you stupid' gesture I knew so well.

"What?" I retorted trying to push her to say it and she did.

"We are not married Cecil Jenkins and only married people sleep together. Especially for one whole week."

I laughed, trying to make fun of her and pretend I didn't mean it that way. "Who said anything about sleeping together? You would stay with…"

She saw through my jocularity and stopped me in my tracks, "Let's forget it," she snapped. "We don't have the money or the permission of our parents anyway. So let's talk about my plans."

"Ok," I shrugged, raising my eyebrows and puckering my mouth feigning disinterest. Dawn was too smart to be taken in by my charade and totally ignored it.

"I told my parents I want to go back to New York for college and they agreed."

"Shock number two in a couple of days," I said sarcastically.

"Why do you say that?"

"Damn," I said, holding my head and closing my eyes tightly.

"What's wrong Cecil?" concern oozed from her voice.

"Why do you have to leave Florida Dawn? I thought we were friends. I thought we cared about each other."

"We are friends Cecil. But I want to become a fashion designer. I love fashion - especially children fashions."

"You don't have to go to New York to do that."

"I don't know of any good fashion school down here, but there is a good one in New York. It's fairly new and everyone is talking about it. The name is…" she paused trying to remember the name of the school, then it came to her. "The name is Fashion Institute of Technology in New York City - downtown Manhattan."

"Why do you have to go to school? Can't you look a fashion job right here in Florida, even in Fort Lauderdale."

"No Cecil, I want to study fashion, not just learn by working." She stared at him a little angry at his lack of regard for scholarship. "This school is expensive but good," she continued, "when you graduate you're more certain to get a good job. Besides, I may even learn about business and, in a little while after I graduate, open my own Children Fashion Store, if I can get enough money."

"Where yuh going to get money to pay for school?"

"My grades are good. I am trying to get a scholarship but even if I don't get one, my parents have promised to make the sacrifice. They told me that if I were accepted they would see to it that I go. The only problem is, it is hard for black people to get into the school. You know how it is -if you are black you have to be twice as good. The school is lily white. I hear only a few black people go there."

"So you want to go to a white school eh?"

"No Cecil, it's not because of white people but it's the only place I know where I can study fashion. I definitely want to do Children's Wear. At the Fashion Institute, the teachers are successful, big time designers themselves. You can imagine how much I'll learn from their years of experience? A friend told me sometimes they have field trips to some of the top designer firms and companies in New York. They even have their own fashion shows.

"You can imagine little me in downtown Manhattan working as a fashion designer?"

She spun around gleefully, her dress twirling in the wind, revealing those gorgeous legs that first attracted me. She was very convincing and I knew she was going to her college in New York. Nothing was going to stop her. She twisted the conversation to me.

"How about you Cecil, which college are you going?"

"College, I not going to no college. I will look for a job downtown and tell stories on Saturday nights." I said boastfully.

She stopped abruptly, a funny look on her face. "Don't you have any ambition Cecil Jenkins? All you want to do is tell duppy stories? And you call yourself my friend. Well you are not my friend. My friends have ambition. They want to go to college, to make something of themselves. No friend of mine ever wants to live off their parents all their lives."

"Live off my family," I shot back disgustedly. "I will get a good job. Yea, and people will come from all over to hear me tell my stories. I might have to get a bigger place and, who to tell, I might even charge them to come listen to my stories. When I am rich you and my father and mother will see. You will see that I am really good and ambitious."

"So your father and mother want you to go to college eh?"

"Err, yes, I suppose so," I said, stammering a bit, not wanting to talk about my parents. But that's exactly what Dawn wanted to do.

"Did they actually tell you to go?" she pressed.

"Yes! That's what I said," I shot back angrily but my fierce answer did not deter her.

"Then why not Cecil? Why not?"

"Because my grades are not good enough and no college will accept me," I replied, finally getting it out of my system.

"You are wrong Cecil; there are schools in New York that will accept you. My father told me the public universities are cheap and will accept people with lower grades. These universities are run by the city and a lot of black folks get in every year. If the Fashion Institute doesn't accept me, that's where I will go. Moreover Cecil, you have one more term to bring your grades up."

"Yea, and what will I study? Accounting? I hate accounting."

"No Cecil, study English, study journalism, or something that will show you how to write your stories."

I thought about it for a while. I would love to go to New York with her. "Ok," I said, "I'll try to bring my grades up and if they accept me in any of the universities in New York I'll go."

She hugged me and I loved it. I enjoyed every minute of the time I spent with her that evening. I planned to pursue all my English courses much more ardently than in the past and made a mental note to speak to my English teacher about it as soon as possible. I went home pleased with Dawn; she was the only one who could make me want to give up storytelling. And yet I was very disturbed at the prospect. Something in my being kept reminding me that I was born to become a great storyteller.

For the next two weeks, I anxiously researched universities in New York with Dawn's help. I learnt I could apply to the City University of New York or Hunter College. Both were public schools and did not cost as much as the Ivy Leagues or private colleges. I also learnt that my grades were not as bad as I thought and could get me accepted as long as I passed my final exams and graduated from Belle Glade High School.

Then one Sunday morning, as we customarily gathered around the breakfast table, I broke the news to my family. I told them I'd try to do well on my final exams and apply for entry to one of New York public universities. They were all very happy; mama beamed the most, daddy was straight faced and Pamela seemed delighted.

"Remember son, learn all di fancy stuff but don't forget you storytelling. Never, never forget it is our tradition," daddy said soberly.

"Daddy!" I said, "I was born to be a storyteller and no matter what, I will always remember to talk about our duppy stories, especially the ones you taught me."

"You know Cecil, I may have let you down. I never really taught you the art of storytelling because you loved it so much and was so bright. You never forget a word of any story I told you. But son, I learn from my grandfather," daddy shook his head sadly, "he was a great teacher, but my father

-your gran'pappy, he was a good storyteller but not a good teacher. Now, I may be a good storyteller but I am like my father, not a good teacher. It is up to you now son, to learn the art in school. I know it will be different but you will be good at it. I know you will be the best."

"Daddy," I responded laughingly, "they don't have a storytelling class in school."

My father laughed loudly too. For a short while, he couldn't control himself, so overcome he was with laughter. When he gained some semblance of composure, he continued: "Cecil, in learning to speak properly, in learning to write properly, in studying how others write stories and books, you will learn all these things and know how to tell a story well. That, my boy, is what I mean by learning the art of storytelling."

"I know daddy, I was just kidding." We both laughed and mama and Pamela joined in the fun.

I left for Jamaica a bright and sunny Saturday in July. Exams were finished and I thought I did well. My application to the City University of New York was mailed and I felt great.

Highgate was great fun, but it was my stay in Kingston that was memorable. Uncle Roger's mother who was not my father's mother had family living on Shortwood Road in Kingston. We spent a week at their house and I met some of the most friendly and beautiful people in the world, especially two sisters who lived next door. They loved my American accent and was happy to be around me. I knew, for certain, one day I would marry a Jamaican girl, hopefully it would be Dawn because I really liked her. But there were so many beautiful girls like Dawn in Jamaica that I was no longer certain that it would be Dawn Cretin.

What amazed me most was the breathtaking splendor of Jamaica. Yes, I lived there for five years but I couldn't remember the place as it was. Sure, I remembered Highgate - a little - especially the house where I used to live, but as much as Florida was beautiful, Jamaica and its beaches outshone it - completely.

As we drove from Kingston along the Junction road leading to my little town of Highgate, I died a thousand deaths. The lush green rolling hills were for real and the banana and cane plantations were simply miracles.

You needed only to look over the precipice at the turbulent Wag Waters winding itself as if in competition with the Junction road as both twisted and turned on their way into the rainy St. Mary hills. Even though daddy had told us about it and gave us glowing descriptions, I was not ready for the matchless beauty I saw. I would not trade the gratification of the two fun filled weeks I spent in Jamaica but, alas, my return to Sunny Florida was inevitable.

I got back in time for the first storytelling Saturday. Daddy, mama and Pamela were now in Africa and Miss Carmen agreed to stay at the house with me. We had decided I should take daddy's place as the official story-teller until his return. At last, I was going to hold my own storytelling night.

Dawn had agreed to remain in Florida just so she could be with me for my inauguration - or so she called it. I said debut. Even though I had told many stories before, this was the first time without my father's watchful eyes. The following Monday, Dawn would be on a plane heading for New York to spend the holidays with her family. She probably would not return to Florida as she expected to be accepted in Fashion Institute of Technology.

I decided to tell a duppy story my uncle Roger told me while I was in Jamaica. The incident took place in '46, just after we migrated. It was about a man named Grant who lived in the district. Neither my mother nor my father knew anything of this story because it happened after they had already left Highgate. When I asked uncle why he did not tell daddy the story when he visited, his reply surprised me. He said my father was far too busy to listen to duppy stories - goes to show how much he knows.

I was very happy to hear this fresh ghostly duppy tale, especially as it was out of Highgate, St Mary. Certainly, daddy wouldn't mind me telling it. After all, it was my story to tell. I mulled the story over and over in my mind getting its familiar feel, noting its nuance, ascertaining its high points and practicing its telling. I wanted to be able to narrate it in the most effective manner. It was my debut and I hoped to make it a great success.

Then, before I realized it, Saturday night rode into our little district and I was sitting on the step daddy usually occupied looking down on the gathering. An overwhelming feeling of power engulfed me. My adrenalin surged; now I knew now how daddy felt. This was what life was all about. I thought about it briefly and agreed that every man should have the sagacity, the wisdom, not just to understand, but to also follow his calling. This indeed was my calling and, by God, I would follow it. I began my story with chutzpa and every man, woman, and child in that crowd felt it, yes; they knew a treat was at hand.

Unlike my father, I did not get to advertise my story, therefore most people were curious about its content. Now they were doubly anxious: will my story be interesting and will I be able to tell it as expressively as my father. I thought of using the first few minutes in an introduction but decided against it. Instead, I told them this was a true story that happened in St Mary, Jamaica in '46, shortly after we migrated. I created a title for my story calling it 'The Dead Little Baby'.

The crowd sat there, facing me, anxious for me to begin. I held my hand up and the place fell silent in the gray evening light. A soft wind rustled the leaves of the nearby mango tree. I delved immediately into my story.

Chapter 9

The Dead Little Baby

*H*alf mile from our house in Harmony Hall, there is a lane leading uphill to an old ramshackle one-bedroom shack. In this shack, lived a young woman named Miriam McBean. Miriam died in childbirth leaving a little girl named after her - Miriam Ann McBean. Before she died, mother Miriam insisted her young child be named McBean because its father had ran away the very day she became pregnant and therefore she did not want any child of hers to get his name.

Young Miriam grew up with her Aunty a few doors away, until she was seventeen and then her Aunt died. After her Aunt's death, she went back to live in the old shack where she was born. Miriam's life was to become entwined with one Joseph Grant, a young man who lived in a little town about four miles away called Richmond. One day, Joseph's mother and father heard he had gone to live in a common law relationship with Maureen Jones, an older woman living in the same district. They were seething with rage the day he visited them. As he entered the living room, his mother approached him.

"What you an' di girl Maureen have Joseph?"

Panic rushed through the young man's guts like a tidal wave. He had no idea his parents had heard. He stared at his mother numbly, not uttering a word.

"So yuh a live wid her?"

Still he remained silent. She moved towards him menacingly. "Joseph," she said, pointing and shaking her crocked overworked finger at the boy who cringed and backed away from her until he was stopped by the closed living room door, "yuh a go bring down shame pan the whole family bwoy?"

"No Ma," he whimpered, pressing onto the closed door, hands held limply across his face, eyes peeping through floppy fingers. The air was steamy as the boy, still cowering from his mother's threatening advance, lifted his hands to protect himself from the vicious attack of her hawk-like hands. A slap landed on the back of his head; he quickly shifted his hands to cover the now painful spot, only to leave his forehead exposed. Quickly, she cracked him with her knuckle on his sweat-covered forehead. "Don't bring nuh disgrace pon wi, mi seh," she squawked, slapping him with every word.

"Damn bwoy, nuh have no sense," his father joined the fray, sitting deep in the massive sofa, looking much like an oversized frog. The living room was small - too small - and packed with extra-large furniture. One could move from one end of the room to the other only by walking along the small pathway left from careful arrangement of the far too many pieces of furniture, vases, carpets, and carvings.

"Yuh nuh shame bwoy? As a Christian, yuh go live wutless life wid dat no-good gal Maureen? Eh?"

He fumbled for the doorknob opened it and dashed out the door. Joseph had been afraid of his parents ever since he could remember. His father was the Deacon for the local Episcopal Church of God while his mother served on the choir and he, against his wishes, dutifully attended church every Sunday and sometimes during the week. He had to get away from it all and Maureen was the answer. Yes, she was nine years his senior but he was twenty-one, which was the voting age; yep he was a big man now.

As he ran down the pathway from his parents' house, his mother's voice rang in his ears, "Don't let down this Christian home bwoy." It was then he made up his mind. He was going to stay with Maureen and never go back to his parents' house - ever.

And so he came to live with Maureen. She was nice, she looked good and they had great times together. As the months passed, Maureen began pressing him to get married.

"Yuh nuh see me a get older an' older Joseph?" she'd say, "when we ago get married, have children, and go serve wi God? It nuh good to live like dis yuh know Joseph." He'd keep quiet, not knowing what to say. He certainly wasn't ready for marriage. And even if he was, he wasn't sure he'd marry Maureen. All his friends have younger girlfriends and they say these young girls were nicer than older women. Maureen was too experienced and behaved just like his mother.

At least once per week, and especially on Sundays, Maureen begged him to decide on a date to get hitched. He never responded. Sometimes she'd get really angry and accuse him of not loving her but it was only when she threatened to leave that he really paid any attention.

"Maureen," he had said, "you know mi love yuh, but wi have to save up enough money first. As soon as me get a good job an' save some money, wi will get married."

This seemed to do the trick because she was perfectly happy with the promise. Except now, she kept tormenting him to find a good job. After ten months of living together, Maureen came in one day quite excited.

"Joseph, Mr. Wilson up a Highgate tell mi fi tell yuh seh, 'im ago start fi buil' a house down a Harmony Hall an' want yuh fi come work wid 'im. 'Im seh is a big job 'im have fi yuh, but 'im wouldn' tell mi nuh more."

Joseph was elated; he enjoyed working for Mr. Wilson, who was a fair man and paid him well. He wondered if Mr. Wilson would remember the foreman job he promised him - and he did.

Two weeks later, Joseph was hired as foreman for the building of a house in Harmony Hall that Mr. Wilson had a contract on. While working each day, Joseph noticed a young lady who never spoke to anyone though she visited the site daily. Each morning, at about nine o'clock, this attractive young girl came to the standpipe by the worksite where she filled her bucket with water and disappeared over the hill. She wore tattered clothing, which refused to hide what he described as her natural beauty, her shapeliness, the glitter in her eyes, the feminine allure of her stride and the pleasant set of her face. Whenever the fellows whistled at her, she responded with a congenial smile. Each day, he felt more attracted to this stranger and couldn't really tell why.

One morning, he approached her and offered to help with the bucket of water.

"Where yuh live?" he asked.

"Is alright."

"No man, mek me carry di water fi yuh."

"Is not far. Me can do it."

"Weh yuh name?"

"Miriam," she answered, holding the side of her skirt, preventing it from dragging on the dirt or getting wet by water splashing out of the bucket.

"Nice name Miriam," he said grabbing the bucket handle stubbornly pulling it from her grip. They walked together along the footpath, up the hill, until he reached her house.

"Dat's where I live," she said, a little ashamed of the small, shackled house she called home. But he wasn't looking at the house and certainly didn't care. The weeks passed and, each day, she appeared and he helped her carry the water home. Soon, they became good friends and he'd stay by her house after work until it got quite late.

His common-law wife kept questioning him about the late hours he was keeping at work but he told her he was playing dominoes with his friends. Normally, she would quarrel bitterly but the money was accumulating in the bank and he reminded her that they would get married as soon as they'd saved enough. By the time the house was finished, he said, they would have enough to get married.

As time passed, Joseph fell deeper and deeper in love with Miriam and she grew to love him equally. She never questioned his other relationships and he offered no information. Then one day, she became pregnant. Joseph told her he would take care of both she and the baby and promised to marry her as soon as he saved enough money. A month after the baby was born, he withdrew half of his savings and took Miriam to see Pastor Ramsey at the Church of the Assembly, where she attended regular service. Pastor Ramsey agreed to marry them and the date was set for two Sundays away.

It was quite an impressive little wedding and every attendee witnessed the love they shared. It was clear Joseph's heart belonged to Miriam in every way possible and she adored him. That night, Joseph did not return to his common-law wife, Maureen Jones. She nearly went out of her mind awaiting his return, but he did not show up the next day either, nor the next. By the following Tuesday, she decided to walk from Richmond to Harmony Hall where Joseph worked. He was hard at work when she found him.

"My God Joseph, what happen? Why yuh nuh come 'ome from Saturday?"

Joseph stared at her without responding then briskly walked towards the large shady mango tree out of the sight and hearing of the other workers. Maureen followed.

"Answer mi nuh Joseph. What 'appen?"

He scratched his head elaborately, "Mi lef' half of di money in a di bank fi yuh."

"Money Joseph? What money?"

He stepped forward to hold her hand; she pulled away and screamed, "What yuh doing to me Joseph. For God' sake tell mi!"

"Mi marry somebody else Maureen," he said simply. Her shoulders went limp; she shook a little, and then pitched forward in a dead faint.

When she recovered he was fanning her with a piece of cardboard, a drink of water in his hand and the workmen gathered around staring down at her. Slowly, she drank the water and stood up.

"Yuh gwine pay fi dis Joseph, yuh an' whoever yuh married to." She staggered away and trudged slowly up the road towards her house in Richmond. Joseph stood watching her go with sadness in his heart, his fists clenched in the frayed pockets of his old cotton trousers.

For three weeks Maureen cried, unable to eat, sleep, or perform any of her normal duties. Then, the Monday of the third week, she put on her good clothes and took the train to Troja. At the train station, she caught a taxi to the house on the hill where Backcross, the renowned obeah man, lived. This was not one of his busy days so she was ushered into his presence immediately. She told him her story.

"So what yuh want me to do?" he asked, once her story was ended.

"Me want 'im back," she said, tears forming rivulets on her thickly powered face.

Slowly, he lifted his head as if in deep concentration, eyes riveted on a distant spot over her right shoulder. The transfixion lasted seconds, then without moving he closed his eyes and spoke coarsely in a thinner voice than usual: "That cyaan 'appen."

"Why?" she hollered, "tell mi why."

"Dem love each odda too much. Di 'oman have fi dead first."

"Den kill her. I don't care. Kill di wicked 'oman. But mi haffi get back Joseph. Mi cyaan live wid out 'im."

For the first time, the short, black obeah man looked at her, his eyes as colored as his teeth.

"Yuh know wha' yuh a ask me fi do?"

"Yes! Mi seh kill her and mek Joseph come back to me. Mi really love 'im," she wailed, "mi cyaan do widout 'im. Everyday, mi feel like me a go dead."

"How much money yuh have?"

Maureen took out the bundle of money she had withdrawn from the bank that morning. Over twelve pounds was there. The little black man took the money and counted it. When he was finished he left the room disappearing behind a curtain leading to his temple and magic laboratory. He picked out a one-dram bottle and placed pieces of white and red roses, dried skullcap tuned with chrysanthemum stone and linden. "Good fi stress and peace of mind," he said to himself. Then, he added dried Vervain aligned with Spectrolite. Reaching deep into a shelf, the obeah man carefully lifted a Quartz Crystal and placed it beside the bottle.

After a few words of Hebrew, turning around and beating the ground with his staff he returned to Maureen, the bottle and crystal in his hands.

"Go home," he said, handing the bottle and crystal to her, "and when yuh tek off yuh shoes put di crystal in di right foot an' leave it dere for three hours. Den tek it out an' keep it pan yuh dressa. Drink every drop a di liquid in a dis yellow bottle. Nothing will bother you after dat. Leave di res' to me. Within a month Joseph will come back to yuh and dem ago bury likkle Miss Miriam McBean. Dis I promise yuh."

"How yuh know her name?" Maureen asked surprised.

He laughed, "Backcross know all t'ings man. Jus' go home and keep quiet. Nuh tell nobody."

She left feeling a little better. That night, she slept well for the first time in weeks, content in the thought her Joseph would soon be back.

As soon as Maureen left Backcross mixed two potions, one for Joseph and the other for his wife. For Joseph, he blended a potion A Ylang Ylang with Lavender Blossoms and Lady's Mantle Blossoms. Then he aligned it with Rose Quartz and Amber. The little obeah man used this frequently to open the heart. He was sure this would make Joseph love Maureen again.

Once he was finished with the potion for Joseph, he sat and thought about the best way to deal with Miriam. Should he call on the hoards of Lucifer to torment her until she shriveled and died? No, he thought, it would take too long and Joseph may get another obeah man to counteract the duppies. The answer came to him as a sign while pondering the question. He was poking around in the dark cupboard and overturned a bottle of Tansy Oil. "That's it," he said, "poison."

Backcross placed a few drops of the poisonous Tansy oil in a miniature dish and added a few drops of Dumbcane juice, then dropped the tip of a small pin in the mixture. The man walked outside where he made a small fire and boiled the mixture and pin making certain he stayed on the opposite side of the smoking fumes. After all the liquid had vanished, he allowed the vessel to cool, pushed the pinhead through a small piece of paper and smiled.

Two days later the wicked man was on his way to Harmony Hall. After Joseph pulled off from work that evening, a stranger walked up to him and asked if he was the foreman for the lovely structure being built. The proud young man not only confirmed that fact but also boasted how he believed he could build a similar structure given the chance.

"Mi would like fi buil' somet'ing smaller pan piece a land weh mi buy," said the stranger.

"Then come back tomorrow an' talk to Mr. Wilson," Joseph invited.

"Maybe if mi tell yuh what mi want yuh can discuss it wid 'im and when wi meet tomorrow 'im we kinda know what mi want."

"Alright," said Joseph.

"Mek we fin' a place fi have a drink an' talk nuh."

They went to the nearest bar where the stranger ordered a double drink of White Overproof Rum for himself.

"Weh yuh a drink" he invited.

"Same t'ing man."

The stranger pulled a vial from his hip pocket and, when Joseph was distracted, poured a small amount of its content in his drink. The men spoke of a two-bedroom possibility on a piece of land in Highgate. After two more drinks, he thanked Joseph and promised to see Mr. Wilson tomorrow. The half-drunk young man went to bed very pleased with the evening's activity.

At a few minutes past twelve, the same stranger approached Joseph and Miriam's little shack. He walked up to the door and rummaged around. Then he found what he wanted; Miriam's pair of slippers she left at the doorstep. Carefully, he pushed the piece of pin, boiled and soaked in poison, in the toe of one slipper, replaced it and went away. That morning, when Miriam pushed her foot into the shoe and experienced a slight prick on her toe, she didn't even flinch. She never gave it a second thought.

During the night, after breast-feeding their little baby, Miriam felt a little woozy and told Joseph. The feeling soon faded and they went to bed, placing the little tot between them on the bed. At five in the morning, Joseph awoke startled by Miriam's screams. He pulled himself up and grabbed her.

"What happen Miriam?" he asked, frightened. His wife's pupils were dilated, her face as pale as death. She tried to talk but only a gurgling sound escaped her purple lips. She felt a terrible burning in her mouth and throat and began to vomit. With lightening speed Joseph grabbed his pants and headed for the door, but as he looked back he knew it was too late, Miriam lay prostrate on the bed.

Joseph pulled the cover off his little girl and it was more than he could bear, his baby girl was purple and swollen in death. Despite his stoic exterior, deep inside Joseph was a kind and loving soul. He broke down and cried for hours. They found him there, hugging his loved ones, crying uncontrollably.

During the days that followed, Joseph experienced some of the worse stomach cramps he had ever had in his entire life but, like everyone else, he blamed it on mourning for his wife and baby. Soon it also passed.

In those days, in the Jamaican countryside, all it took to determine if a person was deceased, was a physical inspection by the local doctor, very rarely was autopsy necessary. After the doctor declares death the dead person is placed on ice and buried at the shortest possible date, normally three days time, or the nearest Sunday. The doctor inspected Miriam and told Tom he suspected she died from poisoning mostly because her lips had turned purple - a sure sign of poisoning. He said the baby had sucked on her contaminated breast and poisoned herself also. No one could guess how Miriam was poisoned and rumors of all kinds passed amongst the people of Harmony Hall. No one, and certainly not Joseph, suspected Maureen as the cause of both deaths.

Three days later Miriam and her little one were placed in a coffin, the baby resting peacefully at her side, and buried behind the house, beside old Miriam, her mother. That night, despite his terrible grief, Joseph thought of Maureen and longed to see her. He fought a compulsion to seek solace from her. After all, he thought, she would not want to see him. Besides, it was no time to be thinking of another woman when his wife was not even cold in her grave. He went to bed alone.

The following evening at dusk, Carol Sadler was attending her shop as she usually did every day at this time. Her husband was out back playing dominoes with his friends so she was alone. She watched as a woman wearing a long dress, and head covered with the scarf, approach and wondered why this woman covered most of her face in this heat. The stranger entered the shop and pointed to the last bottle of cow's milk remaining.

She placed a shilling on the counter and waited. Carol gave her the milk and threw the shilling among other coins in her till, then rummaged through the small change on the ledge above the till for change but when she turned around the woman had already left, she saw her walking through the door and down the street.

"Your change lady," she yelled but the stranger never looked back. Her eyebrows knitted in puzzlement. She swore the money made no sound, no familiar jingle when it hit the other coins in the till. She looked and there was no one shilling piece on top of the other coins. The shopkeeper shook her head smiling and dismissing the incident, saying it was just her imagination. She told her husband about the incident that night and they both laughed, "I must be getting old and losing my mind."

However, the next day at the same time the same woman appeared. Again, the woman pointed to a bottle of milk, placed a shilling on the counter and walked away. This time Carol watched as the shilling hit the side of the till, floated among the other coins without a sound and disappeared before her very eyes. She ran shouting to her husband, "Bee! Bee, di same 'oman weh mi a tell yuh 'bout yesterday, mek wi go catch her."

He jumped from his chair, leaving his game and dumbfounded friends to join his wife in a dash after the strange woman but she had disappeared.

"What happen Carol?"

"Bee, di same 'oman come back, she dress di same way and buy a bottle a milk wid a shilling, but di money disappear as soon as me put it inna di till. Den she disappear to."

This was no longer a joke to the couple. Bee knew his wife was not joking; he could see the seriousness of her behavior and detect the fear in her voice.

"I will stay in di shop wid yuh tomorrow jus' in case she come back."

"Me have a feeling she a go come back, Bee."

He rejoined his friends in their domino game and lied to his friends when they inquired as to what was going on. He said a strange woman purchased a bottle of milk and did not pay but they couldn't catch her.

The following day at the same time, Carol and her husband watched as the veiled lady approached. She paid for the milk with a shilling and walked away. Bee dashed after her shouting for his wife to stay at the shop. The funny thing was, no matter how fast he ran, the lady remained the same distance away from him, he could not bridge the gap between them and yet she was never far away and never seemed to be running.

Then he realized she was floating in the air and moving towards Joseph Grant's one room shack. He followed her past the house and towards Miriam's grave. The woman stepped on the grave and disappeared.

Bee stopped in his tracks, blowing like a mule from his hectic ordeal. It was now almost dark and he didn't know what to do. Just standing before the two graves gave him the shivers. Normally, he was not a fearful man, especially when it came to duppies - but this was different. He was about to turn away when he heard it; a weak crying like that of a baby. Then he heard footsteps and spun, Joseph stood there looking at him.

"What yuh doing here Mr. Bee?"

Bee stammered not knowing what to say, and then the sound came again, this time a little louder, just loud enough for both men to hear it. A terrible feeling gripped them both and they looked at each other wondering if it was real. Joseph dashed to his house and pulled a fork and shovel from their resting place. Both men dug feverishly until they hit the coffin containing Miriam and her baby girl. The sound came again, a baby crying inside the coffin. Frantically, they cleared the coffin and opened the lid. There beside the body of Miriam, Joseph saw his little baby girl, eyes open, crying softly, sucking her finger. Beside the baby lay three empty milk bottles. Overjoyed, Joseph picked up his child realizing she was very much alive.

When Bee and Carol told Joseph the story, he cried like a child thanking his wife for saving their child. Yes! His dead wife had bought milk and fed the baby, and then the duppy had led them to her rescue. The poison had merely placed the child in a coma, which wore off, in the cold atmosphere of the grave.

Though Joseph was united with his child, each evening after work, a feeling of emptiness pervaded his entire being and then he'd feel a compulsion to call on Maureen. One night he had a strange dream. Maureen and Miriam were fighting and Maureen pulled herself from Miriam's grip grabbed Joseph's little baby and broke her neck. A feeling of hatred washed over him and he awoke sweating and terrified. Since that night he never wanted to see Maureen again.

Maureen Jones searched for and listened to every bit of information about Joseph and his family. At first, the news was very pleasing and she quietly thanked the obeah man. Then she heard about the miraculous recovery of the baby and was angry. After all, Joseph still had not returned to her. That Sunday, she went to see Backcross to find out why Joseph had not come back to her. The wicked obeah man gave her a small blue vial half filled with liquid, telling her to drink it before going to bed and in three days time Joseph would be back.

"But what 'im going do wid di baby?" she asked. "Me nuh want no baby weh a nuh fi me in a my house." Backcross sighed and gave her another vial and instructed her to give its contents to the baby, the vial was also blue.

"No one will be able to tell what kill her," he said. "She will die peacefully in her sleep."

That night Maureen, anxious to get Joseph back, drank the contents of one of the blue vials. The next day they found her stretched out on her bed, two blue vials on the night table. Maureen had died peacefully in her sleep.

I finished my story to a standing ovation, the second such salutation ever in the annals of the Jenkins storytelling. I trembled in delight, wishing my entire family was here to witness this wondrous outpouring of appreciation and approval. I bowed low and gracious but they didn't know the gesture was in deep gratification to my lovely Dawn sitting in the front, beaming and clapping supportively.

My God, I thought, now she will surely see this is my calling, my destiny was not studying at some far away university, trying to write some book or other. These people would be here tomorrow and years to come. In the crowd were my friends and many, many other young folks who would be around. Mama, daddy, and Dawn were wrong. Surely, Dawn saw that tonight. I voiced my appreciation as the crowd thinned out and Dawn came to give me a congratulatory hug. I'd have done anything for her to stay and keep my company that night, but, as usual, she insisted on going home, saying it was not proper and, in any case (she said), her parents would kill her if she ever did such a thing.

"But we aren't going to do anything wrong, just talk," I insisted.

"It's not what we are going to do that is wrong, is what people think we may be doing that is disgraceful. Besides," she pointed out smiling playfully, "one thing can lead to the other."

I had no argument against that and agreed to walk her home.

"Yuh like mi story?" I said. It was more of an observation than a question.

Her beautiful head nodded slowly in sincerity, the moonlight streaking through the trees giving rise to shifting dark and bright shadows flickering across her face as we ambled towards her abode.

"It was so real Cecil. Made me believe it really did happen."

"But it did," I said emphatically, "At least my uncle said so. He knows these people and they are still living in Harmony Hall. The little baby is a big girl now. She still lives with her father who has built a much bigger house now."

"You can't be serious."

"But is true. Anyway Dawn, you realize storytelling is my calling though?" It was definitely a question shakily asked, seeking approval.

"Yes Cecil, you are good. No one can deny that."

"So yuh will go to a University in Florida an' mek we stay together eh?" I asked unsteadily, anticipating the worst.

She spun, extricating herself from my grip, eyes blazing like fire in the black night. Then she spoke, a nasty hinge attached to every burning word.

"You crazy shit," she spat, cursing in my presence for the first time, "you t'ink a going give up my life, my future fo' a worthless no good like you... who can't even look a likkle bit in di future? Can't even see dat no matter how good yuh be, yuh a go turn wuckless because no future not into storytelling in Belle Glades?"

It was the first I ever saw her like this, the first she has ever spoken to me in raw patois, cursing and all. She was as angry as a bull but I was even angrier.

"A who yuh a call wutless eh? Unno t'ink unno know everyt'ing. Well, me a go show unno. Me nah lef' yah, an' mi ago mek somet'ing of miself - unno will si," but she was gone, running towards her doorway trying to hide the tears pouring down her gentle cheeks, disappointment twisting her heart, her very soul.

Mixed feelings pervaded my heart as I strode home that night. I couldn't bear the thought of not seeing Dawn again but my heart welled with pride and determination as I envisioned success after success telling stories, people pouring in to hear me, paying lots of money just to hear one of Cecil Jenkin's stories. Yes I'd rent a building and advertise my duppy stories. I'd put out posters promoting next story night and they'd flock to the building, packing it to the brim. People would talk about me. Cecil Jenkins' the greatest duppy storyteller ever, they'd say, and Dawn would travel all the way from New York to congratulate me. She'd come back and meekly acknowledge that she was wrong and I'd marry her. Let her go now, later I'd show her. I went to bed with dreams of grandeur, of untold success but with a quiver in my heart - my one and only Dawn was gone. Little did I know I'd not see her again for a long time and definitely not as I had imagined.

They came back a week later, mama, daddy and my little sister who had lost a lot of weight and looked quite charming. Once they settled in, the stories came pouring out. They all felt Africa was nothing like they'd expected. Ghana was much, much more beautiful than they could ever dream, ripping away images of muscular, sparsely covered black men, half-naked women carrying baskets of ground products on their heads and replacing them with romantic images of times gone by. Gone were the images of bamboo huts and yard animals mixing with playing children. Gone, and replaced by modern building dotted with magnificent churches and mosques, busy streets and vibrantly flowing commerce. From my father, I learned that Ghana was once considered the major place in the world for gold, ivory, and slaves when the mighty Ashanti Empire occupied the area. He said it was the finest and most advanced city in Africa during those times. The people were so sophisticated and powerful that they employed many Europeans as administrators, clerks and workers, businesses flourished and scholarship abounded. After the Europeans colonized Africa, Ghana was the first African nation to win back its independence, albeit barely two years now, in 1957.

My mother relayed tales of Ghana's slave holding, vividly describing its picturesque legacies of colonial forts strung along the coastline. It was in these forts where our forefathers were held before being shipped off to the new world of cruelty, rape, murder and mayhem.

While the forts were heart rending, to my sister, the area's outstanding beaches were compelling, undeniably awe-inspiring, and, according to her, 'simply glorious'. Just listening to them invoked a yearning in my gut to find a way to experience Africa myself - an impossibility I quickly acknowledged. I relied on these snippets of information to fill the desire.

Then it was my time to bring my family up to date on my trip to Jamaica and the goings on while they were away. They listened attentively as I gave them details of my trip and ended with a glorious version of my debut storytelling night. Daddy beamed when I mentioned the standing ovation.

"Were there many people there?" asked Pamela.

"More than at any of our other storytelling nights. The lawn was full with people standing and sitting everywhere."

"Great mi bwoy," beamed daddy clearly pleased, "maybe now yuh can tek over from mi."

It was when mama asked about Dawn that a shadow crept across my face exposing the sadness I felt in my heart and it was then I decided to tell them of my decision to carry on the tradition.

"I'm not going to college, I declared, I'm going to stay right here and tell duppy stories. Everybody loved the story. I know I will do well..."

"Lawd have his mercy," screamed my mother. "Cecil you must be joking. After we agreed that you were going to college in New York, yuh jus' change like green lizard, eh? Listen to me boy, stop you foolishness and plan to leave for New York as soon as the summer is over, you hear me bwoy?"

I looked at daddy for some support and found it in his eyes. The old man's eyes watered a bit and he hung his head in resignation. I needed his support and shouted, "Daddy talk to mama fi me nuh. Mek her understand fi me nuh." I pleaded desperately. The old man held his head up and said, "Isabel let the boy get him chance. Give him a chance."

"Have mercy Lord! Everybody crazy? Cecil you work so hard and pass your exams, you going to give all that away?" At that moment, my little sister spoke for the first time.

"But Ma, Cecil can always go to college next year or some other time if it's not working out."

I wanted to kiss her. I wanted to grab and hug her. With one of her loudest sighs, Mama sunk into her chair and resigned herself to the inevitable defeat of three against one. So I didn't go to college and my dear Dawn was accepted in Fashion Institute of Technology.

The months went by without a day passing that I did not feel the sadness in my heart. I met and dated a number of girls but Dawn never wrote. I just couldn't be serious about any other relationship. I worked at Dillon Hardware as a warehouse supervisor and attended to our once a month storytelling nights. Daddy was getting weaker by the days and left it entirely up to me to tell the stories while he joined the audience, beaming as my voice resounded through the trees and across the skies with sinister tales of duppies and murder. But to my consternation the crowd did not swell, as I expected, instead it dwindled as the younger folks found other things to do on weekends. I too began enjoying the many parties the younger folks were throwing and the movies got more interesting as time went by.

Daddy became weaker and weaker then one Sunday, over two years after she left, Dawn turned up at our house. It was the spring of 1960, one day before my twentieth birthday. The seven o'clock Sunday morning sun beamed through the big mango tree sending strands of radiation streaking across her coffee colored face like an aura of goodwill. I stood, my mouth ajar, my heart pounding almost making visible dents on my chest. She smiled, "How are you Cecil?" I didn't answer, just stared at the lovely lady standing before me. "So I am not welcome here," she laughed.

"Dawn," I mumbled, "didn't expect to see you."

"I know," she said simply, "it's spring break and I thought I'd visit, especially as I heard father Jenkins was not doing so well. I wanted to see him."

I smiled, once again composed, "Come on in."

She stepped through the door as mama and Pamela came from the kitchen to investigate. They hugged, glad to see each other. Then we took her to my parents' bedroom where daddy was resting. After the customary greetings, we left daddy and Dawn alone. I went outside to gather pepper for mama, leaving Pamela and mama to attend to the kitchen.

As we were leaving, daddy held Dawn's hand and said in a weak voice "I'm glad to see you." He wanted to know how she was doing and wanted to know everything she could tell him about New York.

Later, Dawn told me she noticed a sadness appearing on his aging face as he motioned her closer and whispered. "Young lady, I made a very big mistake, I should have sent Cecil to college. You are right and my wife was right. Storytelling is dying just as sure as I am dying. Just didn't want to believe it. And now, I have destroyed my only son.

"But maybe you can help. He will listen to you, if it's not too late. Is it?"

"No father Jay," she had responded, using her favorite name for him, "Cecil can still go to college. He will have to apply again even though he was accepted a couple of years ago. But they will accept him again. I'm sure."

"Then talk to the boy for me. He likes you and will listen to you more than anyone else."

She laughed lightly, twitching her fingers, staring at her fidgety hands resting in her lap. "I'll talk to him father Jay but I don't know about him adoring me, or if he will even listen to me."

"Just talk to him," the old man said, "I know he'll listen to you." He sunk his head in the pillow, worn-out by the strenuous effort of talking to Dawn. She realized this and got to her feet.

"Rest father Jay. I'll be here for another week or so, staying at my parents down the road, I'll see you."

Dawn came into the kitchen as I walked in with the scotch bonnets. The smell of fried salt fish sautéing on a bed of onions, scallion, thyme, and garlic filled the kitchen.

"Staying for breakfast?" Pamela's eyes challenged Dawn to stay.

"Yes man. Is banana and dumpling we having wid di salt fish?" Pamela declared.

"And calalloo to'." I said, proudly holding up a bundle of calalloo I reaped from my own garden.

After breakfast, Dawn asked me to accompany her downtown Belle Glades. We chatted all the way and she told me of the exciting things that were happening to her at Fashion school. She was doing extremely well. She was at the top of her class and she looked forward to opening her own fashion shop as soon as she graduated. She turned to me seriously and said, "Cecil, how's it with you. Everything all right?"

"Everyt'ing' good," I said laconically.

"You sure?"

"Yep."

Dawn sensed I did not want to discuss it and left the subject alone. We spent much of the day shopping and returned at the close of day. I knew she was the girl for me that very night as I said goodbye to her at her old house. We kissed passionately and she was gone.

We spent every minute together on my birthday. She told me she had made many friends in New York but could find no one like me; I was in her thoughts all the time.

"Dawn," I said, I think of you every day. I'm glad yuh come back, even if it is only fo' a visit."

"But I'd like us to be close Cecil."

"Me too."

"Then let's be friends as before," she said.

I knew I wanted her to be my girl more than anything else but I had blown my college chance. I didn't know what to say.

"I know how it is." Dawn held my hands forcing me to face her in an eye lock. "You don't want to tell me but storytelling isn't going as well as you thought. Right?"

I nodded my head, wordlessly.

"Cecil I spoke with father Jay and he said he made a mistake in not encouraging you to go to college."

The tears were close to my eyes now, so I hung my head in an attempt to hide them. I knew for months now that daddy blamed himself for me not going to college but he never actually said it. I didn't want the old man to pass away without seeing me as a successful person. When I felt comfortable enough I looked up at Dawn dry-eyed, "my father shouldn't blame himself. I made my decision, not him."

"I know, but you can still make him happy. Apply to the City University of New York again."

I laughed bitterly, "What difference will it make? I been out of school for a while now."

"It doesn't matter at all how long you have been out of school. If you qualify they will accept you."

"But I am twenty now, too old to be studying. And how will I pay for it?"

"Mother Jay said she and your daddy have a little savings to help you whenever you want it."

I shook my head unbelievingly. A lump was in my throat again. With parents like these, how could I go wrong? I knew it then. Nothing, nothing short of death, could stop me from going to college. I would make my parents proud.

Before she left, Dawn helped me fill out the application. That summer, I received my acceptance letter and started classes at CCNYU. I majored in journalism where a brand new world was opened to me. I learned things I never imagined but mostly I learned to write stories.

Daddy passed away a year after I graduated and I published my first book of duppy stories. His smile and tears were enough to make me know he was a happy man comfortable in the decision he made for his son. My duppy storybook chronicled the history of the Jamaican storyteller, it reported the works of my grandfather and great-grandfather but it told the story of my father, the greatest storyteller of them all. Mother was as strong and as supportive as she had always been and my little sister Pamela studied nursing. My wife, Dawn Jenkins, became a successful fashion designer and was by my side to accept congratulations from my publisher.

Yes, Dawn had taken me all the way from stubborn boyhood to accomplished author and storyteller. Together, we would walk, hand in hand, into the future - another story to be told another time.

Glossary

A:	Can be used to mean "is" /"are" or "have"/"has", "was"/"were"
	"Weh yuh a go?" means "Where are you going?"
Ahoe:	Used to signal a realization (as with "Oh").
Anodder/ Anodda:	"Another".
Awright:	"Alright".
Bodder/ Bodda:	"Bother".
Cho:	Similar to the use of "whatever" in American lingo or sometimes used as an expression of annoyance.
Chu:	"Through." Sometimes this word is pronounced as "tru".
Cyaan:	"Cannot".
Di:	"The".
Dis:	"This".
Fi:	"For".
Gwaan:	"Go and".
Gwine:	"Going to".
Har:	"Her".
Ile:	"Oil".
Ketch:	"Catch".
Likkle:	"Little".
Laas:	"Lose"/ "lost".
Mi:	My, Me, Mine (depending on use).
Mek:	"Make".

Nah:	"Not" or "No".
Nuh:	Can mean know or can be used to emphasize certain actions, commands (eg. "Do it nuh man", "Feed the pigs nuh man").. Can also mean "no" or "don't".
Odder/ Odda:	"Other"
Pon:	"On".
Ramp (v):	Another word for horseplaying.
Raw Chaw:	unrefined or delivering something "just as it is".
Sanky:	Colloquial expression for "song".
Seh:	"Say", "said", "told".
"Him tell mi seh...	means "He told me that" or "He said that"
"Weh yuh seh?"	means "What did you say?"
Si:	"See".
S'maddy:	"Somebody".
Weh:	"Where", "What" (depending on use).
Wi:	"We".
Wi':	A shortening of "will".

❧

About the Author

Lorrimer Burford holds an MBA (Hons.) from the Keller Graduate School of Management at DeVry University, and is a member of the SIGMA BETA DELTA, an international honor society in business, management, and administration. He has earned a diploma in marketing from New York University and a Bachelor of Science in Mathematics from The University of the West Indies.

A teacher, administrator and marketer, this father and husband enjoys writing the stories that he heard as a child - remembering the good old days and colourful Jamaican culture.

Printed in the United States
32774LVS00007B/94-510